P9-BZS-255

OUT OF HIS LEAGUE

OUT OF HIS LEAGUE

PAT FLYNN

Walker & Company
New York

To Cath

First published in Australia in 2006 by University of Queensland Press
Published in the United States of America in 2008 by
Walker Publishing Company, Inc.
Distributed to the trade by Macmillan

"People Get Ready": Curtis Mayfield,
reproduced by permission of Warner/Chappell Music
"We Shall Overcome": Traditional
"Waltzing Matilda": lyrics by A. B. Paterson

For information about permission to reproduce selections from
this book, write to Permissions, Walker & Company,
175 Fifth Avenue, New York, New York 10010

Library of Congress Cataloging-in-Publication Data
available upon request
ISBN-13: 978-0-8027-9776-6 • ISBN-10: 0-8027-9776-8

Visit Walker & Company's Web site at www.walkeryoungreaders.com

Typeset by Post Pre-press Group, Brisbane
Printed in the U.S.A. by Quebecor World Fairfield
2 4 6 8 10 9 7 5 3 1

All papers used by Walker & Company are natural, recyclable products
made from wood grown in well-managed forests. The manufacturing
processes conform to the environmental regulations of the country of origin.

PRE-GAME

★

chapter 1

Picking up his prom date in a horse and wagon seemed like a good idea, especially when the horse and wagon sat in his grandfather's barn for old time's sake. But Ozzie should have known that Pop would take so long to rig up the equipment and groom the horse that there was a chance Ozzie would miss his own prom.

"Can't you go any faster, Pop? We're running late."

"Can't hear you," said Jack, putting a hand to his ear. Jack had been a stockman for fifty years, so one thing he knew about was horses. He knew they were unpredictable as all hell, which is why he took it easy on the open road.

Ozzie just shook his head.

Jess was waiting outside when they arrived—long red dress, shoes in hand. Ozzie took a sharp breath and a long look before he remembered to jump down and help her up.

Jack turned. "Young lady, you look an absolute picture."

"Thanks, Mr. Freeman."

"Can I ask you a question?"

"Sure."

"What the bloody hell are you doing with my grandson?"

She laughed.

Jack said "giddyap" and they clip-clopped down the road.

"This is so romantic," Jess said to Ozzie.

"You know me, Mr. Romance."

They both smiled, knowing it was a long way from the truth.

As usual there weren't many signs of life on the outskirts of the small Australian town, but it seemed even more noticeable at walking pace—the odd barking dog, car bodies strewn across front yards, chickenless coops with corrugated tin roofs.

Ozzie tugged at the shoulders of his rental tux. The jacket had fit perfectly when he tried it on a month ago, but those hundred push-ups a night must have been working because it now felt a size too small.

Jess put a hand on his leg. "You look nice."

"I feel like a penguin."

"Penguins are cute."

Eventually they made it to the main street, where car horns tooted and kids pointed and yelled hello. They rode under a banner that wished them luck for tonight, and under another one that wished the local football team luck for Sunday.

"Nervous about the game?" asked Jess.

"Not really."

"Think you can win?"

"Not really."

Jack's hearing had improved. "Don't talk like that. I've got money on you."

"How much?" asked Jess.

"A month of Ozzie's wages."

"Yeah," said Ozzie. "About ten bucks."

They pulled up in front of the Returned & Services League (RSL) Club but Jess was in no hurry to get out. She snuggled her head into Ozzie's chest. "Time's going so fast," she said. "I just want this to last a bit longer."

He slipped an arm around her shoulder. "Me too."

* * * * *

Mrs. Allan was still at the front door collecting tickets from the stragglers. "You look beautiful," she said when they walked up.

"Yeah, thanks," said Ozzie.

"I'm not talking to you!" She gave him the once-over. "Although I must say, you don't scrub up too badly, for a footballer."

"Ta, Mrs. Allan."

"And seeing you reminds me, drop over on Monday, will you, love? I've got all the paperwork ready for your big trip."

"Can we not talk about that tonight?" said Jess.

Mrs. Allan touched her arm. "Sorry, love."

In the lobby the girls oohed and aahed over one another's dresses while the boys stirred the hell out of each other over their girly gelled-up hair. Much to the disgust of the student committee, some boys were already pulling down the balloons and sucking in the helium.

"Hey, party people."

Ozzie and Jess laughed.

"You sound like Mickey Mouse," said Jess.

"And you look like him, too," said Ozzie.

Johnno took another drag on the balloon. "Least I don't look like a penguin."

Jess giggled.

"Shut up, Johnno," said Ozzie.

"You both look fine, all right?" Jess said.

"I'm just a little bit better," said Johnno. "Girls better watch out tonight."

"Aren't you here with your cousin?" asked Ozzie.

"Yep." He paused. "Lucky I'm not fussy."

The dinner dance was held in the Sir Thomas Mitchell Room, named after an explorer who discovered much of inland Australia, thanks in part to his talented Aboriginal tracker. It adjoined the Las Vegas Showroom, where a band was tuning up on stage. The back section of the room was curtained off, and from behind came the insistent beeping of the new push-button slot machines, demanding to be fed.

After a longish speech by the deputy principal and an overdone roast, the music started. Some girls rushed over and grabbed Jess to dance. Johnno tapped Ozzie on the shoulder.

"You're wanted in the boys' room."

Some others were already there waiting.

"You got it?" asked Bluey. He was holding a bottle of Coke in one hand, Sprite in the other. "Tell me you got it."

"Boys . . ." Johnno reached down and pulled a small bottle out of his left sock, then another one from his right. "I got it."

There was a cheer.

He unscrewed the caps and tipped the contents of the little bottles into the big bottles.

"Give it here," said Bluey. He had a swig. "*Now* this is a party."

The bottles were passed around and the talk soon turned to football.

"You two were on fire last week," said Hoover.

"Got lucky," said Ozzie.

"Five line breaks and twelve tackles don't seem lucky to me." Hoover didn't play football but he knew a lot about it. He was a stats man.

"If you beat Golda on Sunday you'll be legends," said Bluey.

"Won't be easy," said Ozzie. "They haven't lost all season."

"Don't they have some pro on their team?"

Hoover knew the score. "His name's Gardner; played ten NRL games for the Roosters. Golda flew him up for just enough games to qualify for the finals. Last week he scored four tries."

"He'll be no match for us." Johnno did a little shimmy. "I'll fake one way, slide the other, and step right around him."

"Yeah. You'll do the goose step," said Ozzie.

As the boys were laughing, someone walked in.

"What's going on in here?"

They froze. It was Mr. Penissi, senior math teacher and chief head-kicker of Yuranigh High.

He reached into the trash can and took out two empty minibottles of spirits. "Whose are these?"

No one answered.

He pointed at Johnno and Ozzie. "You two mightn't be at school anymore but I can still boot you out of here tonight. You know that?"

They mumbled something that may have been a yes. Or a no.

"Well, answer the question."

"Don't know, sir," said Johnno. "We saw them, too; we were just discussing what to do about it."

There was a pause while Penissi eyeballed the boys. Only Ozzie and Johnno didn't look at their shoelaces.

"Well, discussion's over," said the teacher. "Hand 'em here." He pointed at the soda bottles.

"What for, sir?" said Bluey. "They're just soft drinks."

Penissi snapped his fingers and Hoover passed him the Coke. The teacher took a whiff. "This smells about as soft as your head, Blue."

That got a few laughs, although not from Bluey.

"And the other one."

Johnno reluctantly gave him the Sprite.

"Because I'm in a good mood I'll let you blokes off with a warning. But if I see any more funny business you'll be outside quick as I can say Jack Robinson. Understand?"

A few nods.

"Have a good night, fellas."

"Shit!" said Johnno when he left. "That cost me twenty bucks!"

"Bloody Penissi, we should slash his tires," said Bluey.

"Yeah," said Hoover, "his Ford's a piece of junk anyway."

"Let's do it!" said another boy called Boof. "We'd be heroes of the school."

Ozzie was leaning against the wall but now he stood up. "Fellas," he said, pointing at the door, "there are girls out there, waiting for us. And this is the one night in our lives that we actually look half-decent. Why waste time on Penissi?"

There was a pause as they weighed up the decision.

"S'pose you're right," mumbled Hoover.

Boof and Bluey grunted and the mood changed.

"Hey, Oz," said Bluey. "You gonna do a *Star Trek* tonight?"

"What's that?"

"Go where no man's been before with Jess?"

The boys jeered.

Ozzie smiled but didn't answer.

chapter 2

It was the last dance, and the two held each other close and quiet until Jess whispered, "Look."

She turned Ozzie so he could see Johnno slouched back in his chair, cradling a glass of straight orange juice.

"What a sorry excuse for a Casanova," said Ozzie.

"Shall we?" said Jess.

"S'pose we have to."

Ozzie yelled and before long the three of them were swaying on the dance floor, Jess in the middle.

They sang together, Johnno on harmonies. The music finished and teachers wandered onto the floor, breaking up couples joined at the lip and shuffling them toward the exit.

"You kids be safe tonight, you hear?" said Mr. Penissi.

"We're not kids anymore, sir," said Johnno.

"S'pose you're not." He put his arms around Ozzie's and Johnno's shoulders. "I know I gave you blokes a hard time at school, particularly you, Johnno. But I hope there are no hard feelings."

"None from me," said Ozzie.

Johnno didn't answer.

"I think it's great that you two stayed around this year," said the teacher. "For the town especially. Best football team we've had in years." He leaned in closer, his breath smelling of mint mixed with something stronger. "But let me give you one piece of advice: don't stay forever. This place will suck the life out of you if you're not careful."

When he'd moved on, Johnno said, "That bloke's drunk on my booze!"

Ozzie couldn't help but laugh.

* * * * *

The after party was at Bluey's place. His dad was one of the few farmers who had access to the lifeblood of the country—water—and lots of it, rising from deep underground where it had laid for millions of years. It was used to grow cotton, and large square bundles of it dotted the landscape, ready for a truck to pick them up in return for a truckload of money. All of Bluey's five older siblings had attended a wealthy boarding school in the city, but Blue was expelled, which is how he ended up at Yuranigh High.

The bonfire crackled and spat, a half-empty keg sat on the back of an SUV, and Bluey, Hoover, and Boof were off terrorizing chickens. On one side of the fire Jess was having a heart-to-heart with Jane Frawley, while on the other side Ozzie sat with Johnno.

"Ready for America?" asked Johnno.

"Dunno. Is America ready for me?"

Johnno sniggered. "Doubt it. One thing I've been meaning to ask you, Oz, how are you paying for it all? It must cost a fair bit."

"Not really. Pop bought the airfare—had to work my arse off for it though. The rest is covered by the group. They have fundraisers, and rich people give them money."

"Wish a rich person would give me money."

"They will, you just have to work for them."

"You sound like my mom." Johnno was holding a stick in the fire, trying to set it alight. "I know I'll have to get a decent job one day; thing is, football's all I'm good at."

"Me too." Ozzie stared at the dancing flames.

"You know," said Johnno, "I reckon we could get picked up by a half-decent team if anyone ever came out here to watch us. Make some real money."

"Heard old Cyril's gonna be at the game on Sunday."

"The Broncos' scout?"

"Yeah."

"We better play well then."

They high-fived.

Ozzie looked over at Jess, who was still deep in conversation.

"She doesn't look too happy, mate," said Johnno.

"Yep."

"What are you planning to do about her when you go?"

A shrug, then Ozzie remembered something and grinned. "Bluey says he's met a few American girls in the city. Heaps better than Aussie girls, he said. He told me if I don't dump Jess I'm stupid."

"Bluey's the stupid one."

Ozzie nodded at that.

"You got a good thing going," Johnno continued. "If I were you I wouldn't mess it up."

Ozzie glanced at his best friend. It didn't sound like him. "Look, Jess is great. You know her as well as I do."

"You better hope that I don't," said Johnno.

Ozzie punched his shoulder. "But don't you ever wonder what's out there? That maybe there's someone, something . . ."

Johnno's stick was burning. He threw it into the fire. "All the time."

chapter 3

Behind the goalposts the Yuranigh players sucked air like asthmatics, their shoulders slumped and eyes down. For eighty-eight minutes they'd busted their guts—and plenty of other body parts—to claw their way into a winning position, and now the football gods had snatched it away without so much as a clap of thunder.

No words could describe how they felt, but that didn't stop Rambling Frank—the biggest and ugliest player on the team—from giving it a go.

"I'll tell you what, Johnno, if that missed tackle loses us the bloody game then you'd better bloody well watch out."

Johnno gave him a look. "Get stuffed."

Frank punctuated each phrase with a stab of the index finger. "Don't tell me to bloody get stuffed. I know where you bloody well live."

"Shut up, Frank," growled Mick. "And get your heads up, all of you."

Slowly, all eyes lifted and focused on their captain. Mick was a pig farmer, but he'd once played State League in the city. "Right," he said. "The key here's not to panic."

The Golda supporters were still celebrating their team's try. Car horns blew and beer cans flew. One landed in the middle of the Yuranigh huddle. Ozzie wondered if there was any beer inside.

Mick ignored it. "We'll get the ball back one more time. Let's make it count. Bash it straight down the guts for four tackles, then I'll make a run down the blind side. Johnno, I don't care what happens, get me the bloody ball."

One of Mick's eyes was half-closed, courtesy of an opponent's fist designed to slow him down. It hadn't. Ozzie knew they still had a chance. Mick had gotten them out of trouble before.

The conversion attempt was waved away by the touch judges, the ref checked his watch, and players jogged into position. Johnno tapped Ozzie on the shoulder.

"Be ready," he said.

"You heard Mick," said Ozzie. "Stick to the plan, eh?"

Johnno flashed a grin. "You know me."

A group of Yuranigh followers bunched together, yelling encouragement.

"C'mon, you gutless wonders. Put in!" roared Jack.

"Free beer if you win!" screamed Wazza.

"Go, Ozzie! Go, Johnno!" Jess shouted.

Mrs. Allan waved her hat in the air.

Yuranigh kicked off and Golda played it safe with one-out runs up the middle. After five tackles their halfback put in a towering kick and the Golda team chased swiftly, trapping the Yuranigh fullback twenty yards out from his own line. The referee took another quick glance at his watch. There couldn't have been more than thirty seconds left.

The dummy-half passed to Frank, who ran hard and straight until three defenders upended him. They rubbed his face in the dirt.

"Tackle two," said the ref.

Sweeping up the ball with his left hand, Johnno scooted from dummy-half, dancing and jigging past tacklers until he was pulled down at the halfway mark.

"Tackle three."

Another forward lumbered a few strides before crashing into a human wall.

"Tackle four."

Receiving the ball, Johnno darted toward Mick on the short side of the field. The Golda captain yelled "thirteen," Mick's number, and two defenders readied themselves for a game-winning hit. Johnno shaped to pass, but then stepped off his right foot and cut back infield. Instinctively, Ozzie accelerated. He'd played so much footy with Johnno it was like he could read his mind.

Approaching the line of tacklers, Johnno dropped the ball onto his boot, which somehow missed a tangle of defenders' feet and was scooped up one-handed by Ozzie, shooting through.

"Go!" screamed the Yuranigh fans.

"Stop 'im!" yelled the Golda supporters.

Ozzie tucked the ball under his right shoulder and scurried over the forty-yard line, his feet skimming across the brown grass like stones on water. He was the youngest player on the field, with a face not yet scarred by fights and harsh sunlight, and looked too fragile to be carrying the hope of a town in his hands.

The rangy Golda fullback crouched low in anticipation, arms forward and palms outstretched, and the cover defense dashed across to help. Ozzie looked left and right, but no support was in sight.

Just before he reached the twenty, Ozzie chip kicked over the fullback's head. The ball bounced forward and appeared to be rolling uselessly over the dead-ball line, but then, as footballs sometimes do, it leaped high in the air, as if jumping over an invisible bar. It fizzled to a halt just behind the try line, and Ozzie, the fullback, and five defenders rushed toward it like it was made of gold.

The crowd held its breath.

Ten yards from the line, Bryan Gardner—a ringer from Sydney—was nearing Ozzie's shoulder, and the Golda crowd erupted as if they were watching the favorite bolt home at the Melbourne Cup.

"Go, Bryan!"

"Go, Ozzie!" yelled Jess.

Gardner's legs were tree trunks and each stride cut into Ozzie's lead. Five yards out, the two jostled for position, and Ozzie was knocked off balance. He felt himself falling, and briefly considered throwing out his arms and appealing for a penalty, but instead he pushed hard against the ground, diving low across the turf. Ozzie landed yards short of the ball but momentum carried him forward. If the ground had been wet he would have slid farther, but it hadn't rained out here for months. As Ozzie slowed, Gardner dived, hands outstretched.

The crowd was silent once more.

chapter 4

Cyril Conroy tucked in his shirt the way men used to—undoing his belt, button, and clip before unzipping the fly halfway down. Shirt completely out then completely in, tight like a sheet on an army bed. He sucked in a breath, gave his pants a final yank, and knocked on the door.

"Any luck?" The coach let Cyril in and shook his hand warmly.

"Not much," said Cyril, tugging at his tie. It was eighty degrees in the Brisbane shade but he wore a suit because it was the way he had been brought up. He wouldn't have been comfortable in anything less.

"Saw some talent though," Cyril continued. "A boy from Cherbourg runs the hundred meters in eleven flat. Watched him score four tries, and that was only the first half."

"He interested?"

"Said he'll think about it. Plays bloody baseball as well. Apparently he's being chased by a Yankee scout."

"Baseball? In Cherbourg?"

"My sentiments exactly." Cyril shook his head. "Did sign a big bloke from Dalby. Six foot, seventeen stone."

"What's that in pounds?"

"Umm. Two hundred ten? Should see his shoulders." Cyril held his arms wide, as though describing a huge fish.

"Skillful?"

"Nah. Flat out catching a cold. But has a bit of go in him and he's only seventeen. Did I mention he's big?"

The coach smiled. Big was always good. "Other definites?"

"Not for now."

The coach nodded. "Keep an eye on the Cherbourg kid. We need some good ones for the future. Any more leads?"

Cyril took a notepad from his breast pocket and held it close to his face. "Got some time for a boy out west— place called Yuranigh. A five-eighth."

"Don't tell me. He's big."

"No."

"Fast?"

"Not as fast as the Cherbourg kid. But there's something about him. Can't put my finger on it."

"Have a go."

Cyril looked up at a print hanging on the office wall, a mountain rising into thick clouds. "Grand Final. Team's down by four. The young halfback rolls it through for our mate, who scoops it up one-handed, kicks over the full-back's head, and races Bryan Gardner to the line."

"Gardner? What's he doing out there?"

Cyril rubbed his fingers together. "Mining money buys more than a pick and shovel these days."

"You'd need a car to race him, wouldn't you?"

"I know. He's lightning. Still, the kid's holding his own until he cops a shoulder and falls, but then slides five yards on his belly, like he's on ice."

"Did he score?"

"Yeah. Got a hand on the ball just before Gardner punched it clear. Saw it with me own eyes."

The coach smiled. "The ref agree with you?"

"Nah. But he had the crowd in his ear." Cyril shook his head. "Best try I've seen in a long time. The kid can spot an opportunity like a pretty girl."

"The halfback doesn't sound bad either."

"Actually he's just as talented, but lazy. I'd only recommend the five-eighth."

"Can he tackle?"

"The five-eighth?"

A quick nod.

"Yeah. He's a tough little bugger."

"Mmm." The coach nodded slowly, thinking about what positions the team needed to fill, not just next season but five years down the track. A good five-eighth is like a general to a football team, and generals aren't easy to find. "Tell me his story."

"Property kid. Eighteen, or thereabouts. His grandfather could play as well—I remember watching him once when I was a boy. 'Mystery,' they called him. There's a girlfriend who's still at school—had a chat with her, actually. Good sort. If I were forty years younger . . ."

"You'd be pulling out your boots and playing for us."

The men laughed.

"So you think he's worth a go?" said the coach.

"Hard to tell. Heard he's off to America soon. Some sort of exchange."

"Probably end up playing for the Cowboys."

"North Queensland?"

"No. Dallas." The coach smiled. "I'll leave it up to you, Cyril. Let Liz know if you want to make an offer."

"Yep."

The two men stood and shook hands. Cyril lingered, his left shoulder stooped from too many tackles gone wrong.

"Something else?" said the coach.

"Yeah." Cyril looked back up at the mountain on the wall. "It's just . . . it's not the same out there anymore. I used to be able to pick raw talent like apples. Now they're all playing bloody basketball, wearing shorts around their ankles and hats the wrong way round."

"*They* call it fashion." The coach put his hand on Cyril's

right shoulder. "Look, you're one of the best. 'No one can spot a player like Cyril Conroy,' that's what everyone says."

"I can still spot 'em. It's talking to 'em that's the problem. Sometimes I think I grew up in a different country from these young blokes."

The coach looked out the window, onto a field with grass worn thin from a long season. "I still think that, deep down, they're just like you and me were. Half-full of themselves and half-scared out of their wits."

"Dunno. These kids seem different. Or maybe it's just me. Maybe I've had my day."

The coach looked back at Cyril. "Enough. We'd be lost without you."

Cyril straightened a little. "I've always said that as long as you want me, I'll keep working for ya."

"We want you."

"Thanks. It means a lot."

At the door he turned as the coach called out, "Things are always changing, but that's not a bad thing. Keeps us on our toes."

"Change is hard for an old fella."

"You're only as old as you act. You might try pulling down those pants a little."

"I'd rather keep me jocks to m'self, if that's all right."

They shared a smile.

chapter 5

Ozzie's last night in Australia began before the sun went down. It was Wazza's shout, and because Wazza owned the pub, by closing time Ozzie and Johnno were missing the dartboard and making drunken promises.

"When you get back I'm gonna be Superman," said Johnno, tapping his gut. "Gonna cut out the booze, the smokes, and put on twenty pounds of muscle, lifting."

Ozzie aimed at the twenty but hit the one instead. "Mate, if you're Superman, who will I be?"

"You can be his mate, Tonto."

Jess lifted her head above the beer-stained green of the pool table. "That's the Lone Ranger."

"No, no, no," said Johnno, loudly. "The Lone Ranger doesn't have a mate. That's why he's called the LONE Ranger."

Jess shook her head and sank the eight ball.

"Let me say this," said Ozzie. "I don't care if you're

Superman or Batman or the lone wolf. If you get fit, I'll get us both a tryout for the Broncos next year."

Johnno looked at him. "You're talking about *the* Brisbane Broncos?"

"Yep."

"How the hell are ya gonna do that?"

"After the Grand Final old Cyril told me they might be interested. I'll tell 'em I'm not coming without you."

Johnno lined up to throw. "Swear?"

"Shit, yeah."

Johnno laughed so hard that the dart missed not only the board but the protector as well.

"All right, boys. Think you've had enough." Wazza pulled the dart out of the wall.

"C'mon, Wazza, it was an accident!" said Johnno.

"Could've happened to anyone," said Ozzie.

The boys laughed again.

"Look after yourself, boy." Wazza shook Ozzie's hand. "Want you back next season, fit as a fiddle."

"One for the road?" asked Johnno.

Wazza ignored him. "And good luck with Jack's driving. You'll be bloody lucky to make it to Brisbane."

Jess drove the boys home. Though the winter days were warm, the night wind whipped off the plains and slapped their faces. They cruised down Yuranigh's main street, which was lined with fat bottle trees dedicated to dead soldiers. Some boys leaned on a parked car and drank out of paper bags. Johnno yelled and the boys called for them to stop, but Jess didn't.

Outside Johnno's house, three dogs circled the car, barking and baring teeth. "Shut up, ya mongrels!" Johnno got out and kicked in the dogs' direction, though in his condition he had as much chance of connecting as throwing a bulls-eye. The dogs kept barking.

"We'll stay in the car, if that's all right," Jess said.

Johnno stuck his head through Ozzie's window. "Mate, can't believe you're going."

"Be back before you know it."

"Did I tell you I'm gonna get real fit while you're away?"

"A few times, yeah."

Johnno looked at Jess. "I've been playing footy with this bloke since the under tens, you know?"

Jess raised an eyebrow. "Yeah, I do. I've known you losers since primary school."

Johnno was undeterred. "Halfback and five-eighth, flair and discipline, black and white. That's me and Ozzie."

"Which one are you again?" asked Ozzie.

"Black." Johnno thought for a second. "I think."

Jess laughed. "See ya later, Johnno."

"Yeah, see ya, mate," said Ozzie.

Jess eased the car into reverse but Johnno banged on the hood and she stopped. He bent down, arms resting on the door. "One thing I wanted to ask ya, Oz. Do you think . . ." He started chuckling.

"What?" asked Ozzie.

Johnno's eyes closed. "Do you think I should've passed it? To Mick?"

Ozzie didn't answer.

"I should've, eh? Lost us the game. But I wanted you . . ." Johnno opened his eyes. "When you score, it's like me scoring too, you know?"

"Yeah, I do." They clasped hands.

Johnno ran alongside the car. "You and me gonna play for the Broncos next season."

"See ya, you crazy bugger," said Ozzie.

"You and me."

"Yeah. You and me."

* * * * *

Ozzie's house was a few miles out of town; past Yuranigh's one tourist attraction—a desert spa rising from the Great Artesian Basin, famous for its supposed healing qualities; past the wheat silo with *GO MAGPIES!* painted across it; over the railway tracks where a freight train and a road train collided last year, leaving hundreds of bleating lambs strewn across the road (the lucky ones died instantly); and down a long, dirt driveway that smelled like cows.

A brown kelpie was there to meet them. Jess bent down and scratched her neck. "Let's go for a walk."

"You talking to me or the dog?" said Ozzie.

"Both."

"I still have to pack."

Jess shook her head. "You leave in the morning and you still haven't packed? You're hopeless."

"I know. That's why I was hoping you'd help me."

"We'll walk first."

It was a crescent moon and the stars shone like fireflies. Even if it had been pitch black it would've been fairly safe walking in the paddocks. There was hardly a tree in sight and most of the dams were empty.

A dingo howled and Jess slipped an arm around Ozzie's waist.

"Scared?" he asked.

"Nah. Cold."

They climbed a ladder to the top of the feed loft, sitting on a platform overlooking the property, legs dangling. From up here Ozzie always had visions of falling backward, into the darkness of the loft. One of his grandfather's favorite horror stories was of the time he'd worked on a farm outside Roma. A migrant worker from the city had disappeared, and they'd all assumed he'd shot through because the work was too tough. Weeks later they found him, buried alive in fine grain.

"So, you excited?" asked Jess.

"Haven't really thought about it."

"What about going on a plane?"

Ozzie shrugged.

"You don't think much about the future, do you?"

"No point. What if the plane crashes?"

Jess punched him. "Don't talk like that."

"Sorry."

A star burned a white trail in the sky.

"See that?" asked Ozzie.

"Yeah."

"Make a wish."

"I already have."

They were quiet for a bit.

"What do you think's gonna happen to us?" Jess asked softly.

Ozzie didn't answer.

"What do you want to happen?"

"What do *you* want?" asked Ozzie.

"I asked you first."

Ozzie thought for a moment. "What I want"—he slipped an arm around her—"is to give you the best kiss of your life."

"And after that?"

"I'll give you an even better kiss."

Jess took a small box out of her pocket.

"What's this?" asked Ozzie. "I didn't . . ."

"It's okay."

Ozzie unwrapped it slowly. He didn't want to drop it, especially from up here.

She helped him put it on, clipping the silver watch tight so it pinched the hairs on the back of his hand. It didn't hurt, though. It made him feel alive.

Ozzie kissed her lips.

Jess laid her head on his shoulder and whispered into the night, "I love you, Oz."

They sat for a long time.

chapter 6

From Western Queensland, all roads lead to a town some-times called Bris-Vegas. People from the far west don't go there often; it's thousands of miles of deep potholes and dumb animals that walk, hop, or fly into windscreens like an endless supply of kamikazes. If people from the out-back do come to their state capital, there are three main reasons.

One is the Brisbane Exhibition, known as "The Show," a chance every August to check out some prize cattle and give the kids a look at the fireworks and the big smoke.

The second is to watch the State of Origin, an annual football war between the cane toads of Queensland and the cockroaches of New South Wales.

The other reason to come to Brisbane is to leave it again.

Outside of Toowoomba, after they'd traveled for hours in silence, Ozzie Eaton suggested they take the toll road. Jack Freeman snorted, as expected. Ozzie knew that his grandfather would rather rot in hell than pay for the privilege of driving on a road, but his plan was to try and swing the Gateway. Near Gatton, Ozzie put money in the ashtray. There was a barely visible lining of gray ash from when Jack had smoked. He'd given it up the day Ozzie had come to live with him.

Jack glanced down. "What's that for?"

"The Gateway Bridge," said Ozzie.

"We're not driving over no bloody bridge."

Ozzie tapped his watch.

Jack ignored him. "The government builds a bridge using taxpayers' money and then charges $2 to drive over the bloody thing. I'd rather rot in hell."

It's $2.40, Ozzie thought, but he didn't say it. Instead he said, "I'll miss me plane."

"Good. More work to be done around the farm."

They both smiled, maybe because there was truth in it.

Ozzie left the money in the ashtray but Jack took the city turnoff, like they both knew he would. Soon, they were engulfed in a sea of cars paddling from one traffic light to the next. Exhaust fumes crept into the cabin of Jack's pickup, making him cough and open the window.

"I played there once, you know?" he said. They were inching past Suncorp Stadium, where the Brisbane Broncos play their National Rugby League games. "Of course it wasn't named after a bloody bank then."

Ozzie saw paintings of his heroes, of football legends with names like Wally and Alfie and Locky, on the outside wall of the stadium that used to be called Lang Park. His grandfather had told him a lot of stories, most more than once. But not this one.

"When?"

Jack's fingers tapped the wheel. "Must have been late forties or early fifties, not too long after the war. Got picked for Queensland Country and we played against Country New South Wales, curtain-raiser for the main game."

"How'd you do?"

"We lost, I remember that."

"Did ya play well?"

"Didn't get off the bench. Had a run-in with the coach."

Ozzie looked at his grandfather.

"Bloody city bloke," Jack continued. "Always talking down to us. The night before was the official dinner. Free booze. I must've had too many, 'cause I told him where to go, all right. Told him the only way I knew how."

"Did ya break anything?"

"Just bruised m' knuckles. Some of the other blokes said if I hadn't, they would've."

"They probably wanted to play."

Jack chuckled and Ozzie shook his head. Maybe now he'd heard all his grandfather's stories.

"A funny thing happened, though," said Jack.

Maybe not.

"In the main game, Queensland was copping a hidin.' In those days the New South Wales clubs, who had poker-machine money behind 'em, bought all the best players. No State of Origin back then either, so year after year ex-Queenslanders would wear blue and beat us. It was bloody sickenin'."

The traffic had cleared but Jack drove as slowly as he talked. Ozzie wanted to tell him to hurry up but knew it wouldn't achieve anything until the story was finished.

"I think it was forty-eight zilch or somethin', and so many Queenslanders were injured that the coach asked if any of *us* wanted a run. Quick as a flash I jumped up. Didn't want to come to the city for nothin'."

Jack gave Ozzie a wink. Ozzie wished he'd look at the road.

"But you wouldn't have been on the roster," said Ozzie. "They can't just let anyone on the field."

Jack snorted. "Could in those days. Besides, the game was almost over so no one cared."

"Did ya touch the ball?"

"My oath. Scored a try."

"You scored a try for Queensland? Pull the other one."

Jack's foot transferred from accelerator to brake and he tugged at the wheel. No power steering in this automobile; it was an antique. Someone beeped their horn. "You calling your granddad a liar?"

"Oh, come on, Pop . . ."

He stopped on the side of the road. The shoulder wasn't wide enough for cars to pass easily and a line began building.

Ozzie laughed in shock. "Pop, let's go."

"Are you calling your granddad a liar?"

Ozzie hesitated. "No. Can we go now?"

"Say you're sorry."

Another hesitation. More beeping.

"Sorry." Ozzie looked away.

Without checking his mirrors, Jack pulled back onto the road.

A few more minutes passed in silence. They were hitting every yellow light and Jack stopped at them all.

"Tell me about it," said Ozzie, finally.

"What?"

"The try."

Jack glanced at the crack in the top left corner of the windscreen, then peered straight ahead. "Chooka Jones, our best player, made a bust in the last minute of the game. Everyone was dead on their feet so I was the only bugger who followed him. Fresh as a daisy, I was. Chooka was pulled down at the ten, got up fast and played the ball, and I stepped past the marker and ran it under the posts."

Ozzie looked at his watch and realized the plane left in forty-five minutes. His ticket said to get there two hours early, which meant he was an hour and fifteen minutes late already. "You think you could drive a bit faster, Pop?"

Jack sped up for a minute, then slowed again. "Funny thing, the announcer didn't know who I was. Kept calling me the mystery man. 'The mystery man scores for the Maroons,' he said. The name stuck and for years people called me 'Mystery.'"

Ozzie spotted a plane. At first he thought it was landing, but then saw that it was taking off. He hoped it wasn't going to America.

chapter 7

By the time they parked (Ozzie knew Jack would have a small fit when he found out the cost of airport parking on the way out) and checked in Ozzie's one bag (luckily the plane was delayed, otherwise he would have missed it), it was time to go. They stood under a sign above an escalator that said Passengers Only.

"What's the difference between an Australian and a septic tank?" Jack asked.

"What?" said Ozzie.

"The Australian's only full of crap after a few beers."

"No. I mean, what's a septic tank?"

Jack shook his head. "Where do I go every Friday night?"

"The pub."

"The rubbity dub. Where's your wallet?"

"In my pocket."

"In your skyrocket. So you tell me what a septic tank is?"

Ozzie smiled. "A Yank."

"Too right, son."

"Any trouble, Pop, call Johnno," said Ozzie. "He'll help you round the farm."

"Johnno couldn't help himself to free ice cream."

"I'll write once a week. If you had the bloody phone on I'd ring."

"Watch your bloody language, son."

They shook hands.

Ozzie stepped onto the escalator and began to sink down. He turned. "Hey, Pop?"

Jack hadn't moved.

"That was a good story you told in the car."

For an instant Jack looked confused. Then he smiled.

"Lang Park wasn't even built till 1960," Ozzie continued. "So how could you have scored a try there?"

The last thing Ozzie saw before Jack disappeared was the smile leaving his face. Ozzie knew what he said was true, but he wished he could have taken it back.

* * * * *

Don't open till on plane

Dear Ozzie,

A card and a Caramello Koala to help you fly. When

you're real high in the sky (hey, I'm a poet!) look down and think of me and I'll look up and smile. You make me smile, Oz. Even though there's a hole in my heart now you're gone, I want you to have a great time in America, I really do. I hope you find what you're looking for.
But I can't wait till you come home. I promise you one thing: I'll be waiting.
Love always,
Jess XXXOOO
PS What's the time?

Ozzie was studying his watch when a screen dropped in front of his face. "Ladies and gentlemen," said an actor dressed as a flight attendant, "for your safety and comfort, we require your full attention."

After learning about emergency exits, oxygen masks, and life vests equipped with whistles, the engines roared and the plane raced down the runway. Without knowing it, Ozzie gripped the seat. The wheels lifted and houses became matchboxes, trucks turned into toys, and like a sucker punch it hit him in the gut that there was no going back. He was leaving Pop, Johnno, Jess, and the only place he'd ever known.

When there was nothing to see but blue, Ozzie tilted the seat back and shut his eyes—trying to make up for the sleep he'd missed last night. By the time Jess had helped him pack it was late, even later after their long kiss good-bye. Promises were made. Ozzie dreamed about it now—not the promises but the kissing. It made him feel better. They lay together while Pop lay in the next room, snoring.

The droning of the plane helped the dream, made it more real than perhaps it was. He tasted her neck, felt her tongue as it worked its way down his chest. Suddenly, there was wetness in his lap. It was so warm it burned his thigh.

"I'm sorry!" said a voice.

Don't be, said Ozzie to his mind.

"I'll get a towel," said the voice.

Good idea, he thought.

He opened his eyes now and saw a flight attendant. She was holding a jug of coffee, surveying the damage. A panicked look spread across her face—perhaps she was already anticipating a lawsuit. "Back in a sec," she said.

Ozzie woke up properly. The girl next to him gave a little smile. "That's one way to wake you up."

She was looking at Ozzie's crotch. A dark stain spread across his jeans.

"Any damage?" she asked.

"It's hot," Ozzie said. "But I should be all right."

The flight attendant returned with a towel. "I'm so sorry," she repeated. "Turbulence. Of course we'll be happy to pay for the dry cleaning."

Ozzie almost laughed. His old jeans had seen a lot

worse than spilled coffee. "No worries." He took a peek at the girl who had spoken to him. He was sure she hadn't been there when they took off. "Where are we?"

"On a plane."

"Thanks."

She smiled. "You've been asleep since I got on in Sydney. Reckon you would have slept all the way to Hawaii if the hostess hadn't tried to decaffeinate your manhood."

Ozzie vaguely remembered the bump of wheels on tarmac but he'd turned it into a dream about driving a tractor. "We stopped at Sydney already? Damn, I wanted to see Aussie Stadium."

The girl laughed. "You going on holiday?"

"Exchange," said Ozzie. "High school in America."

She nodded. "I thought you looked young."

"How old are you?" he asked.

"Seventeen."

"I'm eighteen."

"Yeah, but . . ."

"But what?"

She looked at Ozzie's dirty Dunlop Volley tennis shoes. "Where're you from?"

"Yuranigh. West Queensland."

"So you're a country boy?"

"S'pose."

"Ever been overseas before?"

"No . . ."

"Melbourne?"

"No."

"Anywhere?"

"I've been to Sydney."

"When?"

"A few hours ago."

They smiled.

"Which part of America?" she asked.

"Texas."

She put on her best southern American accent. "Everything's bigger in Texas."

"So I've heard. Where are you going?"

"Los Angeles."

"What for?"

"I'm an actor." She put on an American accent again, but this one was different. "I'm going to be a star."

They talked for a long time. Ozzie was impressed that here was someone younger than he who was leaving Australia on a wing and a prayer. He had a family to stay with and an organization behind him if anything went wrong. And this girl only had a friend of a friend she could perhaps stay with for a few weeks, and the phone number of an agent she'd never met. The fact that she seemed less nervous than he was worried him a little.

"What do you do for fun in Yuranigh?" she asked.

"I play footy."

"You any good?"

"I do all right. You any good at acting?"

She looked him in the eye. "I am."

They were descending now, and first the volcanoes and then the waves of Hawaii came into sight. Ozzie tensed as they rose up at him. The takeoff had been okay, but it didn't feel natural hurtling back at the ground like this. He was glad he'd slept through the last one.

The girl touched his arm. "You okay?"

He nodded.

"First time on a plane?"

He nodded.

It was a hard landing, but the pilot threw the engines into reverse and soon they were rolling down the runway like a bus. "Welcome to America!" a cheery voice announced through the speakers.

"The promised land," said the girl beside him.

FIRST
HALF

★

chapter 8

For an Australian country boy, LA was a trip. A mind trip. After being patted down by security and interrogated by immigration, Ozzie was finally let into mainland America. The first place he visited was the toilet.

It was like walking into another world. First, the toilet somehow knew how to flush itself, and then he couldn't wash his hands because the sink had no taps. He looked at it, puzzled.

"Just put your hands under," said a man in a suit.

Ozzie did, and presto! "Thanks, mate."

"If you want hot water just say 'hot,'" the suit explained.

Amazing! thought Ozzie. "Hot." It didn't work, so he said it louder. "Hot!" It was still ice cold, so he practically yelled. "Hot!"

The guy started laughing. "I'm just kidding, man."

You bugger! Ozzie couldn't help but smile. The suit had got him good.

The girl from the plane was waiting for him and she laughed when she heard about his bathroom adventure. As they waited at the baggage carousel, she touched his arm. "I have to meet my friend in Hollywood and I could really use a hand with my bag."

He had eight hours to kill, so Ozzie figured he might as well have a look around.

Although used to lifting eighty-pound bags of fertilizer, Ozzie strained his right forearm carrying this one. "Why didn't your boyfriend just sit in a seat like everyone else?" he asked.

"Very funny," she said.

A blast of warm air hit them as they walked through the glass doors. Outside, the sky was gray, though it was hard to tell where the clouds ended and the smog began.

The girl paid the driver and they hopped on a bus filled with black and brown bodies, though the Jaguars and Mercedes driving past were nearly all driven by white hands that spent as much time on the horn as the wheel. Despite the traffic and the weather, the girl was nearly jumping out of her window seat. "We're on Sunset Boulevard!"

"But there's no sun," said Ozzie.

"You know how many songs and movies have been written about this street?"

"How many?"

"A lot."

Ozzie was more interested in the signs people held

up beside traffic lights that said, Will Work for Food. It was hard for him to believe. If you wanted a feed in Yuranigh you went to Mrs. Allan's place. She always had a few young runaways or old alcoholics over for dinner. Ozzie had eaten there a few times after his father had left and before his granddad had sobered up, but that was nothing unusual. Half the town had eaten there at some stage.

Ozzie lugged the girl's suitcase off the bus and they walked past glittering shops where you could spend $5,000 on a dress, past dim restaurants where you could eat as much as you wanted for $9.99, and Ozzie saw more fat and beautiful people than ever before in his life.

The girl from the plane disappeared into a department store to look for her friend of a friend, while Ozzie kept an eye on her bag. He was looking up at a billboard showing football players the size of professional wrestlers when a girl with wild hair approached him.

"Got a dollar?" Her voice was soft, her jeans and shoes better than his, but her T-shirt was stained brown and yellow. She was probably younger than Ozzie, but her black eyes seemed old. "I need milk for my baby."

Ozzie had difficulty understanding her. It was like a different language.

"What?"

She pulled out a picture. It was definitely a baby, though Ozzie couldn't tell if it was a boy or girl.

49

"Please, sir. She's hungry. Her daddy left me all alone."

No one had ever called him "sir" before. He was unzipping his wallet when the girl from the plane appeared beside him. To Ozzie's surprise she put one hand around his waist and the other over his wallet.

"I'm terribly sorry. My boyfriend doesn't have any money to spare at the present moment." She spoke with an English accent.

The girl with the wild hair stared at the girl from the plane. Ozzie felt uncomfortable, though the hand around his waist felt warm.

"It's for my baby," said the wild-haired girl.

"Yes, I'm sure it is. An addictive white baby either smoked or injected. I strongly suggest you acquire money from another source."

Ozzie coughed.

The eyes of the wild-haired girl sprang to life. Her voice changed as well. "Why don't you go back to where you come from? Leave America for us Americans."

"My origins don't change the fact you're not getting any money."

"Bitch," spat the wild-haired girl as she left.

Ozzie's mouth was open. The girl had talked so gently, and then . . .

The girl from the plane laughed. "You're gonna be a sucker for American girls."

Ozzie blinked.

"I'm all set, so I s'pose this is good-bye. Give me a hug, will ya?" She kissed him on the cheek.

As he started walking back to the bus stop, she called out, "Oi."

He turned.

"Don't forget you're an Aussie."

"I won't," he said.

"And watch TV 'cause you'll see me on it one day."

"I will."

She waved good-bye.

* * * * *

Ozzie was calmer during his second plane trip, so he noticed more. Escaping the city took forever, but eventually he looked down on America's own outback—the bumpy rocks of Arizona and the wide open spaces of New Mexico. They descended into Dallas, where a jungle of towers rose from the plain, thousands of silver panes reflecting sunlight like mirrored lenses.

Herded outside to wait for a shuttle bus, the hot, dry air sucked moisture from Ozzie's lips and reminded him of home. He traveled the same distance in the bus as he would have if he'd driven down the main street of his hometown and back again, and the bus ended up at another part of the same airport, where a smaller plane left for the West Texas town of El Paso.

As he walked into the El Paso terminal, a voice boomed across the room, "Is that an Australian I see?"

Ozzie approached the tall man, who was wearing pointed boots and a Stetson hat.

"You must be Austin!"

"Ozzie." He shook the man's hand.

"Ossie?"

"Ozzie."

"Well, pleased to meet you, Ossie! I'm Dave Graham, this is my wife, Nancy, and these are our kids, David Junior and Alison."

Nancy's hug surprised Ozzie; he nearly headbutted her. She wore a beaming smile and makeup that almost hid her middle-aged wrinkles.

David Jr. was a few years younger than Ozzie but just as tall, and Alison was entering puberty with a mouthful of braces. Ozzie nodded hello.

"Is this everything?" asked Dave, picking up Ozzie's bag. "Heck, Nancy brings home more after a day in Houston!"

They zigzagged across a carpark until David Jr. finally spotted the family sedan—a Buick the size of a small bus. Whizzing along the highway, Nancy kept turning around from the front seat, saying, "You must be tired, you poor thing," and Dave kept looking in the rearview mirror, wanting to know if Ozzie wrestled crocodiles.

It was freezing in the Buick, but outside it was hot and brown. There were cattle roaming and cotton growing, and the only thing Ozzie didn't recognize was a metal contraption sticking out of the ground.

"What's that . . . thing?"

"That thang," said Dave, "is what keeps Texas runnin'. "

As Dave sucked in a deep breath, Alison slipped on some headphones and David Jr. began pushing buttons on a handheld computer game.

"When the town of Hope first sprung up in the desert it was a lot like hell on earth," Dave said slowly. "We have dust storms here that make you forget there's a sun."

"I know what you mean," said Ozzie. "Sometimes we have so many grasshoppers at home they look like a cloud."

Dave held up his index finger. "But then somebody found out that below Hope was a hidden gold mine. Something dark and powerful that changes the way people live. Something that can make and break men."

"What Dave's trying to say," interrupted Nancy, "is that you were looking at an oil rig."

Dave gave Nancy a frown, then kept going. "When oil was discovered, Hope grew more in a few weeks than it had in fifty years. Our twin city, Denham, got the rich investors . . ."

"Rich assholes, more like it," said David Jr., not looking up from his computer game.

"Watch your mouth!" said Nancy.

"But they are."

Dave continued. "And Hope attracted men known as boomers, who trudged into the desert to get oil and came back with faces stained black. My granddaddy was one of those men."

"So people do all right round here?" asked Ozzie.

"Sometimes, sometimes not. When the price of oil is high we're happy, but during the busts there's not much to be grateful for, besides God and football."

They were passing a field where the thick, green grass looked out of place in the sunburned landscape. Posts at either end stood like motionless men with their arms raised high, as if a gun was being pointed at them.

"Who plays there?" asked Ozzie.

"No one," said Dave. "That's the practice field for our football team."

"The pros?"

Dave laughed. "No. High school. Your new high school."

Ozzie couldn't believe it. His school in Australia had one field, used for practice and games. It was hard, with lots of thorns. "The practice field? Where do they play?"

Dave pointed. Behind the field a concrete stadium rose out of the dirt like a colosseum. "Fits twenty thousand people. Used to pack 'em in like sardines every game. Now, it's only full once every two years."

"When?"

"The Armadillo game. Haven't beaten them in a long time, but darn, it doesn't stop us hoping."

Even David Jr. stopped pressing buttons long enough to look at the stadium.

"We're huge fans. Nearly everyone in town is. Course we'd love it a whole lot more if the Shooters'd win like they used to," said Dave. "Season starts in less than a month, so you've come at the right time."

"How many on the team?" asked Ozzie.

"There's fifty in the squad, eleven on the field at any one time."

"Only eleven out of fifty play? What about the rest?"

Dave laughed. "You looking to try out?"

Ozzie shook his head. "Doesn't sound like my kind of game."

Dave gave his wife a wink. "That's a wise move, 'cause let me tell you, it's tough."

"And there are so many rules," said Nancy. "I've been watching it all my life and I still don't understand it."

"And the footballers here are real big," said David Jr. "You're not small but you'd probably get snapped like a twig."

Alison kept listening to her MP3 player.

"What do you play in Australia: Ossie rules, rugby or soccer?" asked Dave.

"Rugby League," said Ozzie. "A hundred years ago it broke away from rugby to become our first professional football. Now it's the most popular sport in the top half of the country. We call it the greatest game of all."

Dave laughed.

chapter 9

The Grahams' house had two floors, and large manicured yards, front and back. Inside were three toilets, two bathrooms, and five televisions—all connected to cable. As well as a television with fifty channels, Ozzie's new bedroom had a trampoline-sized bed. He resisted the temptation to jump on it.

Nancy called him down for afternoon tea, and David Jr. gave Ozzie his first American lesson. "The secret to good iced tea is loads of sugar," he said, heaping five spoonfuls into Ozzie's glass.

"So it's just you and your grandfather at home?" asked Nancy. She passed over a plate of chocolate-chip cookies.

"Yep."

"What's that like?"

"Not bad. I don't get cooking like this, though." Ozzie took a bite.

"These are straight out of a package," said David Jr.

Alison giggled.

"You'll have to excuse your new brother and sister," said Nancy, frowning. "They're a little cheeky sometimes."

In the late afternoon Ozzie hit the wall, so he went to his room for a nap. He woke bright as a button at three a.m. and crept downstairs to hunt for some breakfast, or dinner, he wasn't sure which.

Dave was on the couch watching a giant, flat-screen television. "Can't sleep?"

Ozzie nodded.

"Join the club. Wish I had your excuse, though."

Ozzie looked at the huge screen. "What's on?"

"Football." Dave pressed a button and the picture froze. "Always football." He turned to Ozzie. "You want to fit in here?"

Ozzie shrugged.

"Then you need to understand what football means to this town. But first, I'll fix us something to eat."

He disappeared and returned with reheated pizza. "Your granddaddy let you drink beer?"

"Yep."

He threw Ozzie an ice-cold can.

"If I bore you, just tell me," said Dave. "My kids do."

Dave cracked open his can and took a swig. "Around here, football's a religion, it's as simple as that. Why, I'm not sure, but I've got some theories. For one it's a team game, and when you live in a place that's God-awful hot and dusty and flat as the desert 'cause it *is* the desert, then you need a team of friends to help you survive. Also, it's a sport where physical strength still means something. People around here don't like hearing about California girly men making a fortune punching keys on some computer. This is the frontier, where men are men if they can throw cattle to the ground and shoot a gun. The fact is, football bands people together, through bad times and bad weather, and the Hope Shooters and Denham Armadillos always were two of the best high school teams in Texas. Denham had a bigger weight room and a better stadium, but more often than not, Hope beat 'em."

"How come?"

"Well, we had Coach Hayes and the tough sons of oilmen. The Armadillos had the sons of doctors and lawyers and oilmen who never spent a day working the rigs, but sat in air-conditioned offices and owned their own airplanes. By the mid-eighties, Hope had won twice as many state titles."

Dave took another drink. "Then integration came along."

"What's that?"

"A law that says schools can't have only white kids anymore. Most of the blacks and Mexicans live on the south side of Interstate 20, and nowadays they're bused to either Hope or Denham."

"Why did that change anything to do with football?"

"This is where it gets sneaky. The black kids, well, they love football, and the Hispanic kids are more into soccer. Now soccer might be big in most parts of the world, but not in Texas. When the boundaries were drawn for integration, somehow most of the African Americans ended up at Denham and the Latino Americans at Hope. Today, Hope has one of the best soccer teams in the district, but when it comes to football, well, we ain't been a force since."

"What about Denham?"

"They're awesome. Pre-season rankings have them at number three in the country. Every October they beat up on us and spend the rest of the year rubbing it in."

"So it was just bad luck?"

"Good luck if you ask the people of Denham. But in Hope there's a saying, 'A Denham judge can't draw a straight line.'"

"What do you think?"

"I honestly don't know. What I do know is that the people of Hope would do anything to have a team that wins like it used to."

Dave pushed a button and the picture sprang to life. A boy in a black-and-white jersey zigzagged through the clutching hands of half a dozen defenders. Both the commentator and the crowd were yelling as he crossed the goal line.

Dave stopped the tape. "That's the last time we won the district championship."

"When was it?"

He thought for a bit. "Too long ago."

Ozzie went back to bed around five, where he tossed and turned and thought of football, and Jess. Sleep had almost found him when the birds started singing, and the habit of rising at dawn to feed hungry cows prevented him catching any more shut-eye.

From his bedroom window he watched the sun rise over identical-looking backyards. Through the spray of automated sprinklers, Ozzie spotted a rainbow.

chapter 10

Ozzie began his time at Hope High in the principal's office. Mr. Fraser, a short man in a cheap suit, shook Ozzie's hand briefly and said, "Howdy. Hope you have a great time here."

Ozzie smiled at the way he said "time," the *i* sounding like the *ahhh* patients make when a doctor checks their throats.

"Anything you need, anything at all," said Mr. Fraser, "just ask Miss Simms. She'll take care of you."

Miss Simms, the school secretary, then introduced Ozzie to his "buddy"—Jose Garcia.

"Hey, amigo," Jose said as they shook hands.

"G'day, mate."

They toured the school. Jose was in no hurry to get to Advanced Algebra 4 so they walked slowly.

"You live nearby?" asked Ozzie.

"About an hour that-a-way." He pointed south. "With the other Mexicans."

"So . . . which are you? American or Mexican?"

Jose thought for a second. "My folks are Mexican, still can't speak English too good. But I was born here, which makes me as American as Yankee Doodle."

"Yankee who?"

Jose chuckled.

Unlike Yuranigh High, much of the school was enclosed, linked by stairs and passageways. They passed the lockers and the cafeteria and ended up at the gym, where pretty girls were giggling and hanging up posters.

"Jose!" said one, waving. "Hi Joey!" said another. He seemed to know them all.

One girl squealed and ran over, all bouncing hair and smiling braces. She wrapped Jose in her arms, hanging on a bit longer than just a friend would.

"This is my girl," Jose said.

Ozzie shook her outstretched hand.

"I'm Braidie," she said.

"Ozzie."

"Pleased to meet you, Ossie. I love your accent!"

He looked around. "What are the posters for?"

"Tonight's the big pep rally. Coach McCulloch is introducing the team."

"The footy team?"

She giggled. "I have no idea what you just said, but your accent is sooo cute!"

She gave Jose another hug and the boys left.

"Nice girl," Ozzie said. "How long you been going out?"

"Actually, we don't date," said Jose. "Braidie's my Hopette."

"Hope what?"

"Hopette. They're like a spirit group for the football team. Every player is given one for the season."

"What? To keep?"

Jose grinned. "She bakes you cookies on Wednesday, makes you posters on Friday, looks after you so you can play better."

"Like your own personal slave?"

Jose laughed. "You're a crack-up, man."

After a day of introductions Ozzie was ready to go home and sleep. He had a headache from trying to remember names, and although he could mostly understand the locals—from growing up on a diet of American TV—most of the locals couldn't understand a word that came out of Ozzie's mouth, so he had to repeat himself a hundred times. But when Jose asked if he wanted to watch football practice that afternoon, curiosity got the better of him.

In the locker room before practice you could smell the testosterone in the air. You could also hear it. An ice-cube flew past Ozzie's head, crashing into the lockers; there was the regular snap of white towels flicking against boys' legs; and one boy rapped, pretending his hand was a microphone.

Jose clapped his hands. "Hey, Shooters. This here's my man, Austin."

Ozzie felt his face turn red.

A boy-giant named Tex slapped Ozzie on the shoulder so hard that finger marks could still be seen that night. Then a kid called Malivai asked Ozzie to "give me some skin." Ozzie didn't know what the bloke was talking about until he had his hand slapped.

Another boy stood buck naked except for a football in his hand. His wide shoulders were pulled back and he wore a smile that could double as a sneer. "Hey Australia, you have washing machines in your country? Those jeans could walk away on their own, man."

A few players laughed. Jose wasn't one of them. "Your brain already left your head on its own, amigo," he said. "A long time ago."

The boy cocked his arm back and threw the football at Jose. It hummed and spiraled before smashing into the locker, missing Jose's head by inches. "You be smart enough to catch some bullets today, amigo."

"Asshole," whispered Jose as the boy turned away, smirking. "You just met our quarterback, Sam Wilson. Superstar of his own mind."

Ozzie didn't whisper. "Where I'm from a bloke like that would be taught a lesson, quick smart."

"Same here," said Jose. "Unless you're the star quarterback."

chapter 11

Ozzie sat next to Braidie in the stands, watching. The Hopettes talked about the players they'd been assigned to.

"Not only is Jose a starter," Braidie boasted, "he's smart. He wants to become a lawyer so he can help his family."

"Why? Are they criminals?" asked Toni.

"No! I mean help them have a better life. Not every family owns their own condo in Aspen, you know."

Toni gave a little smile.

Braidie looked at her. "Who's your player?"

"Kurt."

"Isn't he a manager?"

Toni didn't answer.

Braidie turned to Ozzie, but spoke so they all could hear. "A manager adds ice to water bottles and washes uniforms. He's not a real player."

Leesa tried to stop things getting too nasty. "I wish I had Sam. He's so fine!"

The girls murmured in agreement.

Ozzie couldn't believe anyone would want to bake biscuits for that wanker.

"We all knew he'd go to Unity, though," said Braidie. "She's so purdy."

"Who's she?" Ozzie asked.

Braidie pointed.

On the red running track that circled the oval, long-legged girls in short skirts jumped up and down and waved pom-poms. They leapt and waved at exactly the same time and even wore matching smiles, though it looked like hard work. When they stopped, the girl in front talked to the others, waving her pom-poms around as she did so.

"Unity's head cheerleader and she'll most likely be homecoming queen as well," said Braidie. "She and Sam are dating. They're such a cute couple."

Ozzie took a closer look at Unity. "Purdy" must mean pretty, he figured.

The players were running laps and most looked up at "their" girls and waved. Some were a lot bigger than his teammates back home, Ozzie noticed. On his club team even the prop forwards, who were men, carried less bulk than a few of these blokes who were six feet tall, nearly as wide, and just plain fat.

Others were lean but full of muscle, with wide shoulders, big chests, and narrow waists that showed their six-packs, if they were shirtless, like Sam was. And still others such as Jose were small and wiry, but you could tell they were quick.

After the run the players suited up and split into groups—each controlled by a man wearing a cap and a whistle.

"How many coaches are there?" asked Ozzie.

"Just the head coach and the defensive coordinator," said Braidie. "Our offensive coordinator quit after last season and the school said they can't afford a new one."

"So, two?"

"There's the specialist coaches but they don't get paid much," added Toni. "For the linemen, the wide receivers and the kickers."

"And there's the strength and fitness coaches as well," said Leesa.

Ozzie thought of the Yuranigh Magpies with its one coach, Mick, who was also the captain. "Is there a coach who ties their shoelaces?" he asked.

"Pardon me?" said Braidie.

"A coach who ties their shoelaces?" Ozzie smiled to let her know he was making a joke.

Braidie gave him a blank look. "They do that themselves."

It didn't take long for the defensive coach to start getting loud. He was overseeing a drill where big Tex ran with the ball at top speed while two players ran in from the opposite direction and tried to tackle him. The trouble was none of them could. Tex kept slapping them to the ground like mosquitoes and the coach didn't like it. "You friggin' fraidy cats!" the coach yelled.

"We've got a tackling problem," said Braidie matter-of-factly.

The girls murmured in agreement.

Tex lined up again. He was big and strong and mean, just what you want in a football player. "Come on, you pussies," he said to the next pair, "tackle me! I'm an Armadillo about to score a touchdown."

"Tackle him!" yelled the coach. "Hit him harder! Make him bleed!"

The players hurled their bodies like missiles at Tex, but instead of knocking him down they bounced off like pinballs.

"Their technique's all wrong," Ozzie said.

"Pardon?" said Bradie.

"They're gutsy, I'll give 'em that. If it weren't for those pads I reckon they'd be dead. But if you want to bring a big bloke down, one should go around the legs and the other up high, across the chest."

"Believe me," said Toni, "it's not as easy as it looks."

Tex got through the entire defensive team, twelve pairs, without once hitting the manicured turf. The coach sat the players down and spent a good twenty seconds eyeballing them; it was so quiet you could have heard a loose tooth drop. Finally he spoke. "You know, guys, this is a school that's won six state titles. Six." He counted them on his fingers, using his thumb twice. "One, two, three, four, five, six. We've got a tradition as a great football school. Not a good football school, but a great one. Do you agree?"

"YES, SIR," yelled the entire defense.

"Well, let me tell you what I see this year." His voice became louder now. "A bunch of little BOYS who'd rather hide behind their mommas' skirts than put their bodies on the line."

Most of the players looked down.

"Is this what you want to be? Mommas' boys?"

"No, sir," mumbled the team.

"I didn't hear you!"

"NO, SIR!"

"Because right now, I reckon I could call down some of the girls in the bleachers and they could tackle better than you." The coach pointed at the Hopettes. "And if those girls were to do a better job than you, you know what that would mean?"

Some boys said, "Yes, sir," and others, "No, sir."

The coach continued. "They'd take your place on the team, that's what! And you'd be the ones sitting up there deciding what to wear to the game and exchanging cookie recipes. Is that what you want?"

"NO, SIR."

The coach looked up at the stand. "Let me say this, girls. I know y'all are pretty as pictures, I can see that with my own eyes. But what I want to know is this: can you tackle? Because I tell you right now, I need some people who can tackle on my team and I don't know if these boys can."

Some of the girls gave a nervous giggle.

Then the coach spotted Ozzie. "How about you, boy? I know you can talk to all the purdy girls, but can you tackle? If you can, come down here right now, 'cause I need some players who can tackle on my team."

Ozzie knew he wasn't supposed to say anything. When he made the Queensland primary school team they were down 24–0 at halftime and the big-name coach had tried the same thing; called them girls and yelled and blustered, and the players had hung their heads in shame. The team lost 60–6. Near the end, when Ozzie scored the team's only try, he gave his coach a curtsy. He never made another state schoolboys' team again.

Ozzie stood up. "Yeah, I'll give it a go."

The girls stopped giggling.

"Shush!" whispered Braidie.

Dead silence.

The coach was taken aback but decided to play along. "Okay then. Come on down. Hell, I need somebody who can show these mommas' boys a thing or two."

Ozzie sauntered down the stairs and jumped onto the field.

"What's your name, son?" said the coach.

"Austin."

The coach turned to his players. "You see, team. Even Austin thinks he can tackle better than you, and you know why? Because he's watched you. He's seen how bad you are, haven't you, Austin?"

Ozzie didn't say anything.

"But Austin knows that if y'all showed some heart, showed some pride in the Hope uniform, you could tackle as well as anyone. Am I right?"

Ozzie remained silent.

"So let's try the drill again, and this time, let's remember we are Hope Shooters. Let's remember we are MEN. Okay?"

"YES, SIR."

"Okay?"

"YES, SIR!"

Guys started slapping each other's helmets. Tex jumped to his feet. "Aren't you going to give Austin a chance? He said he could tackle me."

The players laughed and so did the coach. "I think Austin will be happy going back and sitting next to all the purdy girls," he said. "Won't you, Austin?"

Ozzie hadn't walked down there for nothing. "You asked me if I could tackle. I can."

The players who understood him laughed even louder.

"You think you can tackle Tex?" said the coach.

Ozzie shrugged.

The coach dropped his voice, speaking just to Ozzie. "Well, I'd love to let you try, son, but if you get hurt, I'm in big trouble. Why don't you head back up to the stands and enjoy the company?"

"I play footy at home."

"Where's home?"

"Australia."

"When did you arrive in Hope?"

"Last week."

The coach stroked his chin. "And you really think you can tackle Tex?"

"I'd give it a go."

There was a pause. "I suppose we could call it an official tryout," said the coach. "You eighteen years old?"

Ozzie nodded.

"Well then, be aware that as an official tryout this is done of your own free will. If you get hurt, you can't sue the school or us for damages."

"No worries."

By this stage the whole team was listening. Coach McCulloch came over and looked at Ozzie. "You're not that big."

Ozzie shrugged.

"It's your call," said the defensive coach.

Coach McCulloch hesitated, then turned his palms out. "Let him try." Then he added to the other coach, more quietly. "What have we got to lose?"

Tex was told to take off his helmet and pads, to make it fair. Coach McCulloch whispered in his ear, "No matter what, this boy is not to be hurt. Run half-pace and shrug him off softly."

Trouble was, Tex didn't know the meaning of the words half-pace or softly.

The whole team sat and watched, and Jose drummed up some support for Ozzie. "Come on, amigo. Bring the big man down."

Sam Wilson yelled for Tex. "Squash him, man. Make him hurt, Texas-style."

The team started a slow hand clap as Tex walked back twenty yards and then began his run. He tucked the ball under his left arm and wound up like a steam train, and the clapping got faster. Tex was 240 pounds and his huge legs powerful as pistons. There were cones set up ten yards apart, marking how wide Tex could run, but they really weren't needed. Tex wasn't going to sidestep anyone; he was going to run right over the top.

Ozzie didn't tackle like the others. He didn't yell and sprint at Tex like a warrior. Instead, he crouched low and did a split step as Tex approached, making sure he was in the right position.

Tex leaned his left shoulder forward and put out his huge hand to knock Ozzie into oblivion, but both shoulder and hand missed. All Tex felt was something driving hard into his legs, and arms wrapping around the back of his knees like tentacles. He tried to keep his big legs pumping, unwilling to believe that someone of Ozzie's size could knock him down, but he felt himself falling and realized he was in trouble.

Big Tex hit the ground with a resounding thump, and for a few seconds there was silence.

chapter 12

"Hurry up already!" Dave yelled at Alison through the bathroom door. "We're leaving in five minutes, with or without you."

David Jr. walked past barefoot, playing his computer game. Dave snatched it from his hands. "For the last time, polish your boots and put 'em on your feet!"

They all finally piled into the Buick, only to get stuck in a traffic jam a mile from school.

"If you kids had done what you were told we'd be there by now," grumbled Dave.

"I think Dad's got his belt on the wrong notch," said Alison. "It's too tight."

David Jr. laughed. Ozzie did well not to join in.

Dave raised his voice. "I don't need any cheek from you, missy!"

Nancy cut in. "Dave, why don't you tell Austin about tonight? He really should know what he's in for."

Dave glared at Alison through the rearview mirror, then took a breath. "Okay, sure."

Alison mouthed a "thank you" to her mom.

"On the third Monday of every August, the Shooters are introduced in a night called 'The Beginning.' The gym is packed, and the joke is that thieves could steal whatever they want in town tonight, except they're all at 'The Beginning,' too." Dave gave a little chuckle.

Alison rolled her eyes.

"Dave's one of the boosters," said Nancy. "They raise money for the team."

"We fixed up the parking lot at Shooter Stadium. Fits a thousand cars," said Dave. "And there's a trust fund that pays Coach McCulloch's salary, so he doesn't have to worry about teaching classes."

"I wonder what Coach Mac will say tonight?" said David Jr. "He must know this is his last season."

"Coach Mac's a good man," said Dave.

"He just can't coach," said David Jr., turning to Ozzie. "Last year when the team lost forty-nine zip to Denham, there were twelve For Sale signs stuck in his front yard."

"His wife told me they were like stakes through his heart," said Nancy.

"Is the team s'posed to be better this year?" asked Ozzie.

"Nope," said David Jr.

"Yes," Dave said, almost at the same time. "We've got

Sam Wilson, Malivai Thomas, and Tex Powell. All great players."

The traffic started moving and Dave eased down on the accelerator. "And a special recruit," he added. "One who just might make all the difference."

For the first time that evening, everyone smiled.

* * * * *

"Ladies and gentlemen, welcome to 'The Beginning!'" said the announcer. "Before we introduce the team, let's see who's in the audience tonight."

He unclipped the microphone from the stand and walked forward. "Now, if you've ever played for the Shooters before, I'd like you to stand up."

A few people stirred.

"Go on, don't be shy."

Dozens of men slowly got to their feet, Dave Graham one of them.

"And if you've ever been a Hopette or a cheerleader, can y'all please stand."

About the same number of women rose, including Nancy.

"And if you want to play for the Shooters one day, please rise."

Lots of boys jumped to their feet, David Jr. included.

"And stand if you want to be a Hopette or a cheerleader, and go to the best parties in town."

Alison was one of the many girls who accepted the invitation, giggling.

"And get to your feet if you're in the marching band, or if you're a friend or relative of a player, cheerleader, Hopette, or band member."

The announcer waited a minute. "Now look around the room."

Most of the crowd were standing.

Outside, fifty restless boys wore new black-and-white jerseys with the logo of a six-shooter revolver on the front and their game number on the back. Beside each stood a Hopette, also in a new jersey, with a number the same as her player. There was one boy, however, who had a jersey with no number embroidered on its back. He also had no girl beside him.

"The whole town showing up to watch us walk into a hall?" Ozzie said to Jose. "People here must be footy crazy."

"Not the soccer team. Last year they made the play-offs, but never got more than a hundred come to watch. We went five and six, but still got nineteen thousand to the Armadillo game." Jose cuffed Ozzie's shoulder. "So how you doing, amigo? Nervous?"

Ozzie shook his head. "Nah. It's all a bit of a joke, don't you reckon?"

Jose put a finger to his lips. "Don't say that. Not around here. For most of these guys this is the highlight of their lives. Not just so far, but ever."

"Fair dinkum?"

"Fair what him?"

Someone shouted from the door. "Everyone ready."

Boys slapped other boys' hands. Girls hugged each other.

"What about you?" asked Ozzie. "Is this the best thing you'll ever do?"

"It's pretty good. But the day I graduate from law school will be better. And the day I buy my parents a house, better still." Jose ruffled Ozzie's hair. "Break a leg, man."

Set up on the bleachers was a brass band and the "Yellow Rose of Texas" rained down. The team moved to wait behind a giant banner. The band stopped and the lights went out. You could hear whispers in the darkness.

A deep voice echoed through speakers. "Ladies and gentlemen. Put your hands together for . . . the Hope Shooters Football Team!"

The lights burst back on and the band started again. Fifty-one boys broke through the banner and bounced down the center aisle. The crowd stood as one, clapping so hard that when they stopped their hands would be numb. Those close enough reached out and touched the boys.

When the walking and backslapping and hollering finished, the boys sat on chairs facing the crowd. Behind each player stood his Hopette, glowing with pride. The cheerleaders performed their first routine of the year and Unity was thrown high into the air, landing with a smile in the arms of two boys.

The announcer came on again. "A very special welcome to the brains behind Hope football. I give you the Head Coach of the Shooters—Ben McCulloch."

As he walked to the front Coach McCulloch was applauded, although not as enthusiastically as the players, or even as loudly as the cheerleaders. "Thank you. Thank you all very much." He paused. "Last year was a difficult year. This year"—he raised a finger in the air—"will be better."

Jose leaned toward Ozzie and whispered. "That's what he said last year."

"When a team goes through a tough time there are different ways to think. We can get down on ourselves and blame someone, usually the coach." A few smiled at this. "We could even, Lord have mercy, move to Denham." Some people booed and put their thumbs down. "Or"—he raised a finger in the air again—"we can focus on the positives, work hard on our weaknesses, and prepare for the day the Shooters will be a force in Texas football again." The coach looked at the boosters. "And believe you me, that day will come."

He now turned to the row of chairs behind him.

"Ladies and gentlemen, the starting quarterback and team captain, a player who has a real shot at a Division 1 College Scholarship. Make welcome, Sam Wilson."

Sam stood and waved, people whistled and screamed. Unity gave her boyfriend a hug.

"And our other captains: big Tex Powell, a defensive lineman who's gonna rough up some pretty-boy quarterbacks this year, and Malivai Thomas, the wide receiver who can outrun any defense in the state, including the Armadillos."

When Tex and Malivai were suitably adored, the coach introduced the rest of the team. The fifteenth player welcomed was "a senior split end who caught eighteen passes last year and scored three touchdowns." Jose stood up and bowed. "And he's also an honor student," Coach McCulloch added, "which makes him the smartest person on the team, besides me."

As Coach McCulloch introduced the last player, David Jr. dug his fingers into his best friend's ribs, and even Alison gave her friends a look and a smile.

"Our very latest addition comes all the way from Yuranigh, Australia," said the coach. "In fact, he arrived in Texas only last week. But when y'all see him tackle you'll know why he made the team. A senior linebacker, Austin Eaton."

Dave Graham, sitting in his special booster seat in the

front row, turned to his left and then his right. "That's my boy," he said, for all to hear.

There were a few murmurs from the crowd. Perhaps some were wondering how an Australian kid so new to the school could make it onto the Hope football team.

"This is a night of believing, a night of community, a night of tradition," Coach McCulloch said in closing. "Because no matter what, through tornado or terrorism, we'll be here again next year, every year. 'The Beginning' is part of who Hope is. My dream is that we can stop looking over our shoulder and become something even greater than our past."

The band played for the last time, a chest-expanding rendition of the school fight song, and everyone marched out into the thick, warm air, laughing and talking and slapping backs.

chapter 13

Outside, Dave called Ozzie over. "You see those men talking to Coach Mac?"

"Yeah."

"Well, the thin one, Pastor Slipper, runs the big church in town, and the small, chubby guy, Mayor Green, he runs the town. They've both got wives on the school board, which makes them the most powerful people in Hope."

"What's a school . . . bored?"

"They decide things, like what books kids are allowed to read. Violence is okay, but sex, 'specially the homo sort, is not."

Ozzie raised an eyebrow.

"They also choose who gets hired and fired, including principals and football coaches." Dave chuckled. "I'll bet Coach Mac is nervous just speaking to them."

Dave led Ozzie over to the men, who were hunched close, talking intently.

"All that's fine in theory," Coach McCulloch was saying, "but Denham's got a new two-hundred-pound linebacker who can run the forty in 4.4, and a running back who's even quicker."

"Both black guys?" asked the pastor.

Coach nodded. "And you know who we picked up? Five Mexicans and an Australian who I'm not even sure knows—"

"Gentlemen, I don't like interrupting," said Dave, "but there's someone I'd like the mayor and pastor to meet."

Coach spun around. He gave a tired smile. "Well, Austin will be sick of me soon enough, so I'll say good-night."

"We'll be in touch," the pastor said to him.

"Coach, before you go," said Dave. "I liked what you said tonight, about looking to the future."

"Thanks."

"There's one sure way to get everyone looking forward," said Mayor Green. He paused for a moment. "Win."

Coach McCulloch shook his head and left.

The men turned to Ozzie. "I admit, we got a shock to see you up there tonight," said the pastor. "We like to know everything when it comes to the team."

"And we didn't know about you," said the mayor.

"So you play football in Australia?" asked the pastor.

"Not like this," said Ozzie.

"Have you ever watched it on TV?"

Ozzie thought for a moment. "Once. I think it was the Superball."

"Super*bowl*?"

"Yeah, that's the one."

"Do you know what a quarterback is?" asked the mayor.

"Nah." There was a pause. "My best mate's a halfback, though."

Dave chuckled. "Well, that's twice as good!"

The pastor didn't smile. "Good luck, boy. I can't guarantee you any playing time, but I can offer you time in church on Sundays. I'd like to see you there."

"And ask your family and friends to visit you," said Mayor Green. "Hope could do with more tourists."

As Ozzie was leaving, Coach Marcus Wright, the man who had a thing for yelling, slapped a hundred-page book of defensive plays into his hands. "Homework," he said. "These plays have to be memorized by Friday night's scrimmage. Our first game's less than two weeks away."

* * * * *

Ozzie looked at the book when he got home. It was full of Xs and Os and arrows, and made about as much sense as Rambling Frank from the Yuranigh footy team after a beer or twenty at Wazza's pub. Ozzie put the book down and took out the pack of twenty-five postcards that Jess had given him, one for each week. A postcard was small enough to be doable, she said, and the aerial picture of Yuranigh on the front would remind him of home. In the top left corner was the primary school where they'd met, the bottom right his grandfather's farm, where they'd said good-bye.

He thought back to that night, in each other's arms. They were silent, mostly, which was how Ozzie liked it. Things only became confusing when words got in the way, words he wasn't good at using. She had turned and looked at him, before it had come time to smooth out her dress and her hair, before it had come time to leave.

"Girls will want you," she said.

He shook his head and was about to speak when her hand covered his lips. "It's okay, I watch TV. I know American girls are bold and beautiful. Of course I want you to be faithful but that's gonna be up to you. But don't forget, I'll be waiting when you get back. Remember, here." She put her hand on his heart.

"And here."

She put her hand on his other heart.

After his mom died Ozzie forgot what touch was like. Sure, Pop gave him a clip around the ear every now and then, and he did a lot of tackling and roughhousing with his mates, but you couldn't compare it, it wasn't in the same world. A world with a woman's touch was something he craved but had forgotten, so he didn't even know he craved it. Not until he met Jess.

Ozzie sat with pen in hand, but everything he thought about writing sounded dumb in his head. Luckily, you couldn't fit much in a postcard, anyway.

Dear Jess,

So I'm in Texas. It's a lot like Yuranigh, just more people who speak funny. Guess what? I made the footy team. They had a special do for us tonight, it was a cack. I wish you could've seen it.

Miss ya.

Love Ozzie

PS Give Penissi a kiss for me, it might help you pass maths.
PSS Tell Johnno to get off his arse and lift some weights.

Ozzie's handwriting was small and messy. He'd always been in trouble because of it, but when he started scoring tries for the school footy team, the teachers mostly left him alone.

Dear Pop,

How ya going? Any rain on the horizon? If it makes you feel any better it's hot and dry here as well. I saw some cows and they looked fatter than ours, though I didn't see any grass. They must be hand feeding them. I'll try and find out what they use.

Any news?

Ozzie

Ozzie fell asleep with the postcards next to him, in bed, but he didn't dream of Jess or Pop. He dreamed of band music and people cheering. He dreamed of Texas.

* * * * *

The next morning Ozzie asked David Jr. a question. "You know that computer game you've been playing, the football one?"

"Uh-huh," he said, while munching on a Pop Tart.

"You reckon it could teach me how to play?"

David Jr. laughed, accidentally spitting out a piece of fake strawberry.

"Gross!" said Alison.

"You're on the football team and you don't even know the rules?" asked David Jr.

Ozzie shrugged.

He pressed buttons on the way to school, in the backseat of the Buick. "What's third and four mean?" Ozzie asked, reading the screen.

"That means it's third down with four yards to get,"

said David Jr. "You have four downs to make ten yards. If you don't, the opposition gets the ball."

"What's a down?"

"A play."

"Thanks."

By the time they'd got to school Ozzie knew the basics of American football, thanks to a computer game. It made him feel a lot better.

He met up with Jose who took him to his first class. In the corridor Ozzie received more praise than when he'd won the South-West Queensland Rugby League rookie of the year award.

"I heard you knocked down Tex. Way to go," said one boy.

"You the man!" cried another.

All he'd done was make a high school team. In Yuranigh, club footy was decent, but all you needed to do to make the school team was show up.

While they waited for the history teacher, a girl wearing a tight red T-shirt and a matching bow in her hair approached Ozzie. "Hi, I'm Angela, and I've been assigned your Hopette. It's sooo good to meet you!"

She gave him a hug. Ozzie hugged her back. It seemed the polite thing to do. "I'm sure we'll get to know each other real well," she said. "But for now, I just want to know one thing: what's your favorite type of cookie?"

Ozzie didn't have to think. "Anzacs. Bloody love 'em."

"Excuse me?"

Ozzie thought for a second. He gave himself a mental uppercut. "Yeah, I s'pose you don't have those. How about . . . chocolate?"

Angela's huge smile returned. "I make the best chocolate brownies!"

Brownies? Aren't they young Girl Guides? "Sounds good," he said.

She hugged him again and walked off, her ponytail bouncing off her back. *No one should be that excited about making me cookies,* thought Ozzie. Then he noticed her legs, long and shapely. His own girl-slave? It would take a bit of getting used to.

During class, Miss Webb talked about the fight between the Mexicans and the Texans, when the border was in dispute in the 1830s. "The Alamo was where a few Texans sacrificed their lives rather than surrender to the large army led by the Mexican president, Santa Ana. The Texans ended up killing nine hundred before they died, and it was this act of bravery that was said to have inspired others to defeat the southerners."

"Hey, Jose. Remember the Alamo?" said Sam Wilson, making the class laugh.

Miss Webb turned to Ozzie. "Has there been anything like that happen in your country?"

He thought for a bit. "There was this bloke, Captain

Artie Beetson, who led Queensland to victory in the first State of Origin."

"Did many people die?"

"Nah, but there were quite a few casualties."

Ozzie was still chuckling when the bell rang, and students rushed past as Miss Webb tried to yell out homework. The teachers would skin students alive if they tried that at home, Ozzie thought. Out in the hall another girl came up and introduced herself. She looked familiar.

"I just wanted to say hello and welcome to Hope."

"Thanks," said Ozzie.

A voice yelled from down the hall. "Hurry up, Unity!" She ignored it.

"Let me know how Angela works out. Coach asked me to choose a girl for you and Angela's lots of fun. But if she doesn't look after you real fine, come see me."

Ozzie found it difficult to look at Unity without staring. There were pretty girls in Yuranigh, but she was in another league. The American league.

She touched his arm. "Bye, Austin."

Sam was still waiting, his fingers drumming a locker. When Unity reached him he pulled her so close that their hips were joined as they walked away. Unity swiveled her neck and threw Ozzie a smile.

He couldn't help but smile back.

chapter 14

Even though a scrimmage is just a practice game, a chance for the coaches to see who can handle the yelling and the pressure, and who can't, three thousand people still dropped by to watch the Hope Shooters play the Placeville Warriors on the last Friday night in August. As the red West Texas sky turned black, the lights of Shooter Stadium could be seen fifty miles away, from the desert, and the people of Hope were drawn to them like moths.

Both coaches tried to talk the game down, said it didn't really matter too much, win or lose. "We'll be trying to iron out a few of the kinks, that's all," said the Placeville coach. "Just want to get the boys used to hitting and being hit," said Coach McCulloch. But the fans knew it was just coaches' talk, trying to protect themselves in case their team lost.

Long-time Shooters' fans such as Dave Graham, Pastor Slipper, and Mayor Green were looking for the big four. If the quarterback connected his passes to sprinting receivers, if the running backs gained valuable and tough yards on the ground, if the defense rushed the opposition quarterback *and* hit hard on their tackles, it was bound to be a year when the people of Hope could walk down the main street with shoulders back and say, "So, how about those Shooters?"

In the days of Coach Hayes they could walk with shoulders back down the main street of *Denham*—with its fancy shops and glass office buildings—and not have to say a word. The Shooters' shirts they wore said it for them.

If the team was successful in three out of the four, there was potential. If three legs of a chair are strong and one is wonky, a coach worth his salary, like a good carpenter, should be able to fix it, or hide it. Even the Hope State Championship team of '82 had a quarterback who couldn't throw for crap, but he sure could run.

If the team showed weaknesses in two or more legs, it would mean a chair that, if pushed hard enough, would fall to the ground. It would mean a year when the locals would walk down the main street with shoulders slumped and say, "So, how about those Shooters?" in a tone of voice that made it clear that what they really meant was, "Why the hell aren't they winning?"

And tonight, all of that would become clear after forty-eight minutes of football time, which equaled three and a half hours of real time. After the band marched and the cheerleaders, led by Unity, excited the crowd with airborne splits, the players ran onto the field with arms outstretched, pumping up the crowd even more. The referee blew the whistle and the Placeville team kicked off. The season had started.

Ozzie was one of those eleven Hope players on the field, one of the boy gods. Unlike the other ten, though, he didn't know what was going on.

He didn't have to do much, which was just as well, because the bulky pads made him feel like a blimp, and the helmet, apart from weighing him down, acted like blinkers. Unless he turned his neck he could only see one way. Straight ahead.

Malivai was the kickoff returner, and when he caught the ball eleven opponents bore down on him like terriers in the bodies of Great Danes. Hope had a few big players but they were leprechauns compared with these blokes. Ozzie's job was to stop one of them by running at him and pushing him out of the way, which was called blocking. Blocking wasn't allowed in League. If you tried it, you'd get ten minutes in the sin-bin. Ozzie did his job, knocked a bloke to the ground, and got called a "pussy." He smiled, heard the crowd erupt, and looked up to see Malivai bobbing and weaving, floating across the turf like a black Jesus. Malivai made it over halfway before he was shouldered out of bounds.

The cheerleaders cheered even more and the Hope crowd gave him a standing ovation.

"That boy sure can run," Mayor Green said to Pastor Slipper.

"He can sing, too," replied the Pastor, and the two smiled.

Walking off the field Malivai slapped Ozzie on the back. "Good block, man."

"Thanks, Mal."

It was a long time before Ozzie made it back on. Except for kickoffs and penalty field goals he only played defense, and tonight Coach Wright said he wasn't even going to play much of that because he was still learning the finer points of the game. He told him to watch and learn.

Sam Wilson and the offense jumped and pranced onto the field, and on their first drive Sam connected a perfect spiral pass to Malivai, who caught it and ran close to the end zone. The aim of the game, Ozzie knew, was to cross the goal line, same as Rugby League. In League it was called a try, in American football it was called a touchdown, even though you didn't have to touch the ball down on the ground like you did in League.

On the second play a huge Warrior broke through the middle and tackled Sam before he got a chance to throw. Sam was hit so hard that his chin slammed into his chest, which made him bite his tongue, which made him drop the ball. The brown leather egg bounced free across the turf until what seemed like a hundred bodies dived on top of it. This made Ozzie smile. Only one player ever bothered to dive on a ball in League—the first bloke who got there. This looked like a game he and his mates used to play in primary school called pile-up. When the last of the bodies was removed, a collective groan came from the Hope fans. The Warriors had recovered the ball. The Hope fans groaned again a few minutes later when the Warriors' running back busted through for a touchdown. Warriors 7, Shooters 0.

Before the first quarter ended the Warriors kicked a field goal to take the score to 10–0, and they scored again before halftime. Hope had problems, big ones. You didn't have to be an expert coach or a long-time booster to see that.

But Coach McCulloch believed in positive thinking. Every night before he went to bed he read a page of the Holy Bible, followed by a page of his own personal bible, *A Winning Focus*, which said that before you address the negatives you must focus on the positives, so this is what Coach did in his halftime speech.

"Sam, you're throwing the ball real well. You've completed six passes, five to Malivai and one to Jose, and they've all been fine throws."

"I could do a lot more if our line would stop 'em," Sam snapped. "They're worse at protection than a leaky rubber."

Coach held up his hand. Obviously, the kid had never read *A Winning Focus*.

"And Tex, you've made eight tackles," he continued. "That's a great effort."

Tex's head rested between his knees, dripping sweat into a towel. He looked up and nodded.

"And Malivai, what can I say? Great runnin', great catchin'."

Then Coach's voice got louder. "The rest of you ought to be ashamed of yourselves. You are playing like a bunch of SKIRTS!"

The positives were over and it was time to address the negatives. Coach did a lot of yelling over the next ten minutes, about pride, passion, and executing their game plan.

Ozzie knew about pride and passion though he couldn't have executed the game plan if he tried. He didn't know what it was.

"When playing man on split receivers, align yourself with an inside out position and use the red zone in coverage," Coach said. "If we run cover two, then get on the outside shoulder. Bump 'em to the inside, which'll force that receiver to run into deep coverage. IT'S AS SIMPLE AS THAT."

In Yuranigh, when Ozzie's team had the ball Mick yelled "up the guts," and if that didn't work he yelled "spread it wide." And the funny thing over here was, even with the hundreds of complex plays, all the quarterback ever seemed to do was hand the ball off to a running back, who'd run, or pass it forward to a receiver, who'd catch it and run. There were no backline moves, wrap-arounds or switches of play. Nothing like League. Though the Hope players were fast and well drilled, there was more they could do, thought Ozzie. Much more.

The Shooters kicked off in the second half and Ozzie managed to actually make a tackle. He drove in low and hard and knocked the Warriors' big running back to the ground and got called a "pussy." Coach Wright gave Ozzie a pat on the backside as he came off. Ozzie raised his eyebrows. He wasn't used to coaches patting his arse.

Unfortunately Ozzie's tackle didn't matter, because the Warriors scored again to make it 24–0. The Shooter who missed his man was almost tackled himself as he slunk off the field. "How could you be so stupid!" screamed Coach Wright, scrunching up the player's jersey as he made a fist.

The Warriors' offense pointed to their green jerseys as they pranced off, rubbing in the score line to the Hope crowd. The Hope supporters responded by leaving, their only consolation being that this was just a scrimmage, and perhaps the team would turn it all around by next Friday. And perhaps the price of oil would shoot back up to how it was before those crazy Arabs joined together to try and squeeze the good ol' Texas oilmen out of business. And perhaps it would rain, and perhaps pigs would fly.

The supporters who did leave, however, missed the best Hope play of the night.

In American football the scoring team kicks off, so the cocky Warriors lined up ready to charge after their touchdown. Malivai was ready to try and dodge as many tacklers as possible, but the kicker shanked it, the ball tumbling end over end. Ozzie was standing in front of Malivai, ready to block another Warrior and be called a pussy, when the ball bounced on the 40-yard line, kicked up high, and landed right in Ozzie's hands.

"Run!" yelled Coach McCulloch.

Ozzie started off lazily across field, searching for a hole in the opposing line. Suddenly, big Tex knocked down two Warriors with a single block and there was a hole big enough to drive a truck through. Ozzie accelerated. He didn't look fast but once he was in the open even the men who he played against rarely caught him. As he came to the Warriors' safety, their last line of defense, Ozzie could feel a presence on his right, a friendly presence. With the end zone in sight he thought he could probably slide by the safety with a shoulder fake followed by a big step off his right foot, but then thought, why?

"Mal!" Ozzie yelled, right before getting tackled.

Malivai got a shock. He was sprinting beside Ozzie just in case there was another Warriors' player he could block. Actually, he'd been trying to block the safety before Ozzie reached him but the Australian had been too quick.

Malivai had no idea why Ozzie called out until suddenly the ball came toward him.

In the stand, Pastor Slipper threw out his arms in disbelief.

Unity squeezed pom-poms to her chest.

Coach McCulloch dropped his jaw.

And Malivai almost panicked. But when the ball hit him in the heart, his hands wrapped around it like it was made of glass. And to the delight of the Hope supporters still at the game, he carried it all the way into the end zone.

chapter 15

The Shooters lost, 38–14. They let in five touchdowns and scored only two: one a feathery pass by Sam to Malivai in the dying minutes of the game, and the other a freak kickoff return that was shown on Channel 5 local news.

"Quick!" Dave called out, pressing the record button. "Ozzie's on TV!"

"It could have all gone so horribly wrong," said the sports reporter as Ozzie's pass teetered through the air in slow motion, "but some quick thinking by star receiver Malivai Thomas saw this act of craziness result in an unlikely touchdown. Frank, let's hope Coach McCulloch teaches the Ossie a lesson in ball control."

"Indeed," said Frank, a news anchor with more gel than hair. "And tell us, Bill, what do you make of the Shooters' chances against Booth this Friday?"

"To put it bluntly, Frank, not much. The Bears are

bigger and stronger than the Shooters, and Hope'll be facing a hostile crowd down there. If the scrimmage is any indication, Hope's in for a rough season."

"Their fans won't like to hear that. Now, on to the weather, it's going to be hot, hotter, and hotter still . . ."

Dave turned the television off. Everyone was silent for a few seconds.

"What do they know?" said Dave finally.

"Yeah. Just 'cause they're on TV doesn't mean they're smart," said David Jr.

"That's why they're stuck doing local news," said Nancy.

"And they're ugly, too," said Alison.

Ozzie was still looking at the blank screen. It was the first time he'd ever been on TV. "Can we watch it again?"

* * * * *

At Monday's practice Coach McCulloch signaled to Ozzie, who was running up and down stairs with the rest of the defensive team.

"I want to talk about that lateral you threw," said the coach.

"What's a lateral?" asked Ozzie, puffing.

"A backward pass."

"Oh."

Ozzie prepared to get yelled at. Instead, Coach rubbed his chin. "I'm curious. Why'd you do it?"

"Umm, I don't know. At home, we do that all the time."

"I see." Coach McCulloch ran his hand through what was left of his hair. There were black marks under his eyes, and the jumbled thoughts that had kept him up all night still bounced around in his head. The Shooters had lost to Placeville, a team that hardly rolled off the tongue during conversations about great football programs, and the weaknesses had been there like he hoped and prayed they wouldn't. A few weeks ago he could have almost convinced himself that the team's lack of size could be overcome by desire, by speeches about pride, by heart. But size beats pride every time, and if you'd given Coach truth serum before the season he would have told you that this was always going to be a tough year. Just like last season.

"Control the line of scrimmage, men," he'd yelled to his players in the moments before battle. "If we do that we control the game." The team had speed in Malivai and Jose, a quarterback who could throw, and Tex, a big man who could move like a small man, but it wasn't enough. They didn't have enough quick big men to control the line, and if you couldn't do that, you couldn't win. That reporter was right about one thing, the other teams were bigger and stronger than the Shooters, and Coach knew that he could lose trying the same old moves as last Friday, or try something new. It didn't really matter, anyway. Both the pastor and the mayor had called him up after the loss, and they sure as hell weren't offering a raise. Coach knew he was practically a dead coach coaching.

"This might seem like a strange question," he said to Ozzie, "but do you know any rugby plays that might help our offense?"

"It's Rugby League."

"What?"

"I play Rugby League. Rugby's more for the private school kids."

"Okay then, do you know any Rugby *League* plays that can help our offense?"

Ozzie gave him a big smile. "Heaps."

From then on, in the mornings, when the players did endless runs up and down steps and around the field, Ozzie, Malivai, and Jose were excused. The other players grumbled, none more so than Sam, but what a Texas football coach says, goes.

Ozzie started by explaining to Jose and Malivai the theory behind Rugby League. He'd been in America long enough to know it wouldn't be easy. "Us three, we're all the same. I can pass to you, you can pass to me. I can run, you can run."

Jose and Malivai glanced at each other.

Ozzie continued, searching for the right words. "I don't care who does better, I actually don't give a stuff. If I can draw a player and pass to Jose, then he'll go further than me. That's good. Then he'll draw a player and pass to

Mal, and he'll go further again. That's good, too. You see what I'm saying?"

"You're saying that it's good," said Jose.

There was a pause. "Umm. Any questions?" said Ozzie.

"So we're like a triple threat?" said Malivai.

"What?"

"You know, like in basketball."

"I played basketball for the school once. But I didn't know the bloody rules so the ref kept fouling me."

Jose and Malivai looked at each other.

"We're not *like* a triple threat," said Ozzie. "That's what we *are*."

They started trying to put theory into practice. "Pretend it's a giant egg. Look at your target, aim at their chest, and catch with soft hands." Ozzie threw one to Jose, knocking him back a step.

At first, the giant egg would have been scrambled many times over, but soon the boys caught on, and before long it was whizzing from one player to another. They ran up and down the middle of the field, sometimes in a straight line, sometimes zigzagging behind each other.

Coach sent over some young defenders and Jose and Malivai began to sense when the tackler was committed, just by the look in his eyes, and then whip off an inside or outside lateral. Sometimes, Ozzie would play defense and run hard at the intended receiver, trying to break his concentration. It rarely worked. Jose and Malivai had

had tacklers running at them all their footballing lives and were trained to forget that defenders were hoping to smash them in two. They kept their eyes on the ball.

After a few days the boys really started to connect, on and off the field. They ran through plays on napkins in the cafeteria, before cracking up at how Ozzie called ketchup "tomato sauce."

The other players wondered what was going on, particularly Sam. It wasn't easy seeing his two best receivers do something other than catch his bulletlike throws.

He sought out Coach McCulloch. "I'd like to know what's happening to our offense."

"Nothing big," said Coach, not meeting his eyes. "I just want a few tricks up our sleeve for later in the season. Don't worry, you're still our number one man."

* * * * *

"I'm worried," Sam said to Unity, as they lay on top of the water tower that helped keep the animals, crops, and people of Hope alive. "Coach is up to something and it's pissing me off."

Unity was gazing at the horizon. "Look over there. It's beautiful."

Sam didn't. "And that Australian guy, what the hell's going on there? He's in the country two minutes and Coach thinks the sun shines out of his ass."

Unity was still watching the edges of the sky.

"Are you gonna talk to me or what?"

"This isn't about Austin," Unity said. "It's about you having to be the best. Your daddy wouldn't let you be anything else."

"As a shrink you make a good cheerleader."

Unity tried to stand but Sam grabbed her arm.

"Don't walk away," he said.

"Let go of me."

His face softened. "Please?"

"Only if you let go."

He did.

Unity slowly sank back down. "Sam, you know I care about you, but . . ."

"What?"

"I don't know if I need someone who lives their life like there's something to prove."

He sighed. "What *I* know is you love dating the quarterback of the football team, even if you pretend it doesn't matter."

"And you'd still date me if I wasn't head cheerleader?"

Sam shrugged. "But you are. There's ordinary people . . . and there's people like us. We're meant for each other."

She gave her head a tiny shake.

After a pause, Sam picked up a pebble. "You know my dad took me to see Coach Hayes when I was ten years old?"

She looked at him but didn't answer.

"He'd stopped coaching by then but he was still Dad's hero. Mine, too. I let go a few spirals, as hard as I could throw, and Coach bent down to my face. 'You want to be a Shooter one day?' he said. 'Yes, sir.' He pinched my stomach. 'You're gonna have to lose some of this puppy fat, but if you work hard enough, I believe you can do it. That's one heck of an arm God gave you.' My daddy was so proud when Coach said that."

Sam threw the pebble off the tower. It flew a long way. "Not long after, Dad moved up east. He phones every Saturday morning during the season, and the only thing we talk about is football."

"At least you can talk about something."

Sam shook his head. "If I get through this season with decent stats and no injuries, I can get a scholarship to Justice University, and we can go there together. Imagine that, you and me, at college! But if Coach starts pulling me from the field . . ."

"It'll be okay."

"No. It won't. What else am I gonna do? Work the oil fields?"

Unity began stroking Sam's scalp through his thick hair. "Let me take your mind off football."

Sam let his head fall back and finally watched the reds and pinks of the sun as it died another day.

chapter 16

After being waved off by the Hopettes, the players boasted about the mayhem they'd create, at both the game and the after-party. But as they reached the edge of Hope—past the Wal-Mart that sells everything from Bibles to bullets, the Dairy Queen that sells instant burgers and shakes, and Pastor Slipper's church that sells eternal life—it started to sink in that they'd return either heroes or villains, and most gazed out the bus window in silence.

In the stale visitors' change room the players' helmets sat in front of their lockers like alien heads, cleaned by the student trainers so they sparkled black and white. Underneath the bench, white shoes showed no sign of last week's dirt. They were pure and ready to run, almost as if they could do so on their own. Uniforms were folded identically and cups turned upside down, reminding players to think before they drink.

pat flynn

*IF YOU WANT SOMETHING BAD ENOUGH, YOU
WILL BE DENIED BY NOTHING OR NOBODY*

That quote, from *A Winning Focus*, was taped to the
locker-room wall. It made Ozzie smile, recalling how the
only thing ever taped to the wall before a Yuranigh game
was the weekend racing guide.

Otherwise, Ozzie discovered that football players act
in similar ways, no matter where they're from.

In Australia, Rambling Frank liked to pace around
the change room and roar, "Let's smash 'em!" Here, Tex
slapped guys on the chest and growled, "We're gonna kick
some Bear ass!" If the recipient didn't say "Yeah!" he'd hit
him harder and say, "Aren't we?"

Mick was always so nervous before his pregame
speech that he'd usually throw up his ham sandwich.
After that, however, he was as calm as a Samurai warrior.
The day of the Grand Final he spoke slowly and quietly,
like a funeral director. "It's all about the basics, fellas.
We run hard, we tackle hard, we hold onto the bloody
ball. And don't forget your one-percenters." He looked
at Johnno when he said that. "I'm talking about ya kick
chases, about not givin' away no silly penalties, about
backin' up the ball carrier. And if someone's givin' you
young blokes a hard time, let me or Frank know. We'll
sort 'em out."

"Bloody oath!" Frank said.

And that was it.

Before Coach McCulloch clapped his hands and fifty-one boys crouched on one knee to listen, Malivai did the same as Mick. He threw up his hamburger.

"There are a lot of boys who'd love to trade places with you right now," said Coach. "Boys who'd give their left arm to be sitting where you're sitting. But they're not. For one reason or another, you are the men who are going out on that field tonight. You are the men representing our school, representing our town."

Coach McCulloch was a lot more eloquent than Mick. His head made slow half-circles as he spoke, trying to gain eye contact with each and every player.

"Why? Well, for one, you all have God-given talent. But what you do with that talent is up to you. You can question it, you can doubt it, you can roll over and quit and piss it all away if you want. Or else"—Coach put his index finger in the air—"you can trust it. You can use that talent to the best of your ability. You can stand up and be counted and walk onto that football field knowing that, no matter what it takes, you're going to get the job done. And you can play like champions here tonight."

"YEAH!" Everyone exploded into action. Some boys jumped in the air and chested each other; others slapped their own faces, hard. Then they put their hands into the middle and yelled the team's war cry: "SHOOTERS! SHOOTERS! SHOOT 'EM UP, SHOOTERS!"

Ozzie was about to run onto the field when someone grabbed his hand. The team stood in a circle.

"Heavenly Father," Coach McCulloch began.

Praying before a game was something else Ozzie had never done in Yuranigh, though a few of the blokes didn't mind taking the Lord's name in vain. Ozzie followed the others' lead and bowed his head, watching adrenaline-pumped legs twitch and shuffle.

"Give us strength tonight to do our absolute best. Let us believe in the talent you have given us and let us play as well as we can possibly play. We make this prayer through Jesus' name."

"AMEN!"

"One more thing," said Coach McCulloch. "Let's go bust some heads!"

As the players entered the field, Hope supporters stood and saluted their gladiators by waving black and white scarves. The teams lined up and sang "The Star Spangled Banner," and Ozzie was surprised that not only did everyone know the words but they all sang. Loud. Ozzie didn't know all the words to his *own* national anthem, let alone this one.

The electronic scoreboard showed the American flag, but as soon as the referee raised the silver whistle to his lips the flag was replaced by the score.

The game began.

* * * * *

In the fourth quarter, with the scoreboard reading Bears 31, Shooters 10, the game was as good as over. There were positives, of course. Sam had thrown a fifty-yard touch-down pass to Malivai, Tex had sacked the quarterback, and, in a real surprise, Ozzie had made three tackles. After the first half Coach Wright had plunked Ozzie into nearly every defensive play.

Unfortunately the negatives outweighed the positives. The offensive and defensive line had been pushed off the ball, just like they had been last week, and just like they would be next week. The coaches yelled "Control the line of scrimmage!" like a mantra, but they were only words, and words couldn't hold back the Bears, who were bigger, stronger, and quicker.

When the defensive line collapsed and Sam got sacked, again, Coach called him to the sideline. "I'm going to give you a break," Coach said.

"Why?" Sam said. "We're getting killed out there."

"Exactly." Coach put a hand on Sam's shoulder. "I want to save you for next Friday. You're our MVP."

This made Sam feel better, until he saw that his replacement was not the skinny sixteen-year-old backup quarterback who hoped like hell he wouldn't be sent onto the field, ever, but someone who had never thrown a tight spiral in his life. Or a loose spiral, for that matter.

It was Ozzie.

Sam ripped off his helmet and threw it at the ground.

Coach wasn't planning on using these Rugby League plays until later in the season, if he used them at all. But now he thought that there wasn't much to lose and he could find out once and for all if Malivai, Jose, and Ozzie would be better off running up and down stairs and around the oval in the mornings than underarming a football to each other.

The change was announced over the speakers. "New quarterback for the Shooters, number twenty-two, umm . . . I can't find him. That's not his name, ladies and gentlemen, we'll get back to you on that."

Dave Graham held up mini binoculars. "That's Austin!"

"What in God's name is going on?" asked Pastor Slipper.

"An Australian as quarterback!" said Mayor Green. "The sooner this coach goes the better."

Dave looked over, surprised. This was the first time he had heard anything about getting rid of the coach from someone who actually had the power to do so. He'd heard the rumors, of course, but the fact that the mayor was saying it out loud, here at a football game, meant it was for real. Coach McCulloch may as well start packing his bags.

Ozzie, of course, didn't hear any of this. He was more worried about having to stand directly behind the center—the player who bends over and snaps the ball back to the quarterback—with his hands up the bloke's backside.

"What play we running?" asked Curtis Riley in the huddle. Curtis was an offensive lineman whose job was to run at the player who stood a few inches in front of him. The guy in front of him tonight was seven inches taller and twenty-eight pounds heavier so it wasn't the most fun Curtis had ever had on a Friday night.

"Well," said Ozzie slowly, looking at the linemen, "you blokes stop those bastards from tackling us." He then turned to the two Shooters' receivers. "And you two, run any way you want." They looked at each other. "We know what to do," Ozzie said, indicating Jose, Malivai, and himself.

"What's the blocking formation?" said one of the offensive tackles.

Yesterday, when Ozzie finally found out the names of all the positions, he thought it was funny that there were two players called tackles who weren't allowed to tackle.

"Just . . . do whatever you want."

Curtis let out a stifled laugh. "Good luck, dude."

A whistle blew.

"When's the snap?" the center yelled to Ozzie as they ran to the mark.

"The what?"

They lined up in an unusual way, with Jose and Malivai standing in a diagonal line to Ozzie's left. The Shooters' fans sat up in their seats. Till then, Dave Graham knew every offensive formation the team ran. In fact, the offense had hardly changed in thirty years, which was the way the people of Hope liked it.

"They're going to run left!" yelled a Bears' linebacker.

Ozzie waited for the center to pass him the ball. "All right, chuck it," Ozzie said finally. But the center didn't hear him.

A whistle blew. "Delay of game!" said the referee, moving the ball back five yards.

The Shooters' fans groaned.

"This is embarrassing!" said the mayor.

"A disgrace!" said the pastor.

The players went into a huddle again. "When's the snap?" the center asked Ozzie.

"Whenever you want, mate," said Ozzie.

"How about on three?"

"Fair enough. Who counts, you or me?"

"You."

Curtis laughed again. "Good luck, dude."

They lined up in the same formation as before, with Ozzie, Jose, and Malivai making a line across the left side of the field.

Instead of saying "Hut, hut, hut," Ozzie said "One, two, three," which made the defensive tackle laugh so hard that snot came out of his nose and hit Curtis in the helmet. The center snapped the ball back, Ozzie grabbed it, and he ran.

He angled left across the field and to the Bears' surprise there was no lead blocker. No one running in front of Ozzie, smashing into would-be tacklers. Eleven pairs of eyes lit up as they prepared to destroy an easy target.

Swarm the ball! were the words they had heard all their footballing lives, and that's what they did now, intending to crush Ozzie like an insect. But right before the sickening sound of flesh on flesh, Ozzie did something they weren't expecting. He sent a long, crossfield, Rugby League–style pass to Jose.

"They're running the option!" yelled the Bears' linebacker. The option was a play rarely seen in high school, as it was considered too risky. The safety slid across the field to meet Jose, who had already made enough yards for a first down.

Up in the stands the Shooters' fans were cheering. This was something good in a night of mostly bad. But as Jose was about to be tackled, something more unusual happened. In fact, it was so unusual that the radio commentator told the Hope listeners that in thirty years of watching football he'd seen it only a few times. The ball was passed backward again.

When Malivai caught Jose's pass there was nothing but artificial daylight in front of him. And no one could catch Malivai from behind. He ran it in for a touchdown.

In the stands, the Shooters' crowd was caught between

cheering and stunned silence. For one thing, the game was already lost, but also they knew it must have been luck. A fluke, like the touchdown Malivai scored in last week's scrimmage.

But if you hadn't spent a lifetime watching American football—like Pastor Slipper and Mayor Green—you would have sworn it was the perfect play, and that it was all planned.

chapter 17

After a postmatch drink where they had to listen to the Booth mayor and pastor crow like roosters, Mayor Green and Pastor Slipper drove home in the pastor's Cadillac. The speed limit was fifty-five miles per hour on the interstate but the mayor knew all the police by name, so the pastor set the cruise control for sixty-five.

"So, what's it gonna take?" asked the pastor.

"At least fifty."

"Fifty thousand to fire a lousy football coach! What's this country coming to?"

"You know, if he was abusing a player we wouldn't have to spend a cent."

The pastor thought for a bit. "I don't think anyone'd believe it. If he did beat up one of his players occasionally, we might actually win."

"We could accuse him of discrimination?"

The pastor shook his head. "The team's full of Mexicans. Heck, he's even got an Australian playing quarterback."

"A white Australian."

"Yeah, but . . ."

"You're right. We'll have to get the cash."

"Is it possible?"

The mayor stroked his chin. "Anything's possible."

"How much is there in the boosters' coffers?"

"About twenty, I'd say, ready for a new set of jerseys or an end-of-year trip or whatever. They'll part with it if the bait's tasty enough."

"And the other thirty?"

"It'll have to be the school board," said the mayor. "Christ, they just spent a hundred Gs trying to figure out why our test scores are so pathetic."

"What did they come up with? That the students are stupid?"

"Something like that." The mayor chuckled. "I think they can spend money on something really important."

"Like a new football coach?"

"You got it."

The men smiled.

"But we do nothing until we've found a replacement?" asked the pastor.

"Yep. 'Specially now the season's started and all. It's gonna take the right name to persuade 'em."

"I got an idea about that."

The mayor flicked his Zippo and lit a cigarette.

"Who's the one person that the whole town worships?" said the pastor.

"Jesus Christ?"

The pastor shook his head. "Someone better."

"I think you're getting pretty close to blasphemy there, Pastor. Unless you're talking about . . ."

"Yep."

"Coach Hayes? The man's sixty-four years old."

"He won a hundred and twenty-eight games and lost eighteen. I don't care if he's a hundred, he knows how to win."

The mayor didn't look convinced.

"With him on board we could raise a million dollars if we had to, and McCulloch will be coaching junior high in Oklahoma where he belongs."

Mayor Green blew smoke out of a crack in the window. "And if Hayes is past it, we get rid of him after the season. Tell him it was just a caretaker's role."

"Exactly."

"It might just work. But why would he do it?"

"There's gotta be something we can offer him," said the pastor. "A statue in town, rename Shooter Stadium after him when he dies . . ."

"Both'll happen, anyway."

"What about money?"

"He doesn't give a damn. All he cares about is pride and glory."

"Then we tell him God and the town need him. That here's his chance to make Hope great again. That the people of Denham are laughing at how bad our team has become."

"They *are* laughing."

"We can visit him together."

A siren sounded and a car with red and blue lights pulled onto the highway behind them.

"Do we need a police escort?" asked the mayor.

They smiled.

chapter 18

Wednesday was always hard-work day, the bumps and bruises of last week's game forgotten, and the bumps and bruises of this week's game still far enough away not to matter. It was full contact, players blocking and tackling each other with the abandon of those too young to know the long-term impacts of regular body collisions. More important to them was competing for a place in the starting lineup, for to be a starter on the football team was to be a star. And after the Booth game there were plenty of positions up for grabs.

It had already been decided that Tex would now play both ways, in other words, he'd be an offensive *and* a defensive lineman. This meant he had to be superfit, which was not a word that came to mind when you saw him. To get him ready, Coach Wright had Tex hit anything that moved, and if the boy slacked off just a little bit, Coach'd have him hit the ground and do fifty. Push-ups, that is.

Like many of America's football coaches, Marcus Wright was an ex-military man. "Training for a football game," he often said, "is not all that different from training for a war."

The only other person to play both ways was Ozzie. A month ago he didn't even know the rules and now he was the backup quarterback and a key tackler.

Toward the end of the session the offense was scrimmaging against the defense. "Blue nineteen on three," said Sam in the huddle. "Ready?"

"Hold on," said Malivai. "I've been running at Ozzie all afternoon."

"So?"

"He tackles hard, man. Why don't you run at him for once?"

Jose laughed.

"Okay, girls, I will. Get ready to see an Australian knocked on his butt."

Curtis sniggered and Sam raised his voice. "Just block your man for once in your life and I'll show you how this game should be played."

Although Sam was a throwing quarterback, he could run when he had to. His size—over six feet tall, 180 pounds—allowed him to bust tackles, or he could use his impressive agility to beat them. He play-faked to Malivai—who ran through the middle with his fists curled up in his jersey—and hooked back right, his arm cocked so the defenders would hang back for the pass. Unfortunately for Sam, Tex didn't hang back for anybody, breaking through the designated blocker like he was made of paper. He charged like a wounded bull, and at the last moment Sam jumped back and to the left, and prayed. Tex fell for it hook, line, and sucker, but he stuck out his huge hand on the way past and got hold of Sam's jersey, spinning the quarterback like a top. Somehow, though, Sam ended up on his feet and facing the right way, so he took off toward the secondary defense. Toward Ozzie.

The playbook called for Sam to slide feet first into an incoming tackler once he ran over ten yards, which was enough for a first down. The idea was to protect the valuable quarterback from injury. Sam had run at least fifteen yards by the time he reached Ozzie but he had no intention of stopping. It was time he taught this Australian a lesson about football—Texas-style. Since Sam had been a boy he'd been groomed for this. His father had taught him more than how to throw a football, he'd taught him *football*. Every play on television, every practice session would be analyzed like it was the most important thing in life.

See the open man? That's where you throw, son.

Poise under pressure. You have that, you win football games.

Sam was ready for his time in the sun and now a boy from halfway across the goddamned world was trying to rain on his parade. This boy didn't understand the game the way Sam did, hell, he hardly even knew the rules, much less the playbook. He didn't have a father who'd drummed it all in, then left.

Suddenly there was an enormous crunch, the sickening sound of two bodies colliding.

Sam had to be helped up.

"Sorry, mate. You all right?" Ozzie grabbed Sam's shoulder.

Sam held his head, as if trying to keep his brains from floating away. "Get your hands off me, faggot."

Ozzie raised his hand and his eyebrow. "Mate, lose the attitude. If you were half as good as you think you are you'd be Wally Lewis."

"You calling me a Wally now?" Sam didn't know that Wally Lewis was the Joe Montana of Rugby League.

"I'm calling you a wanker."

Sam stepped closer and took off his helmet. "A what?"

"A wanker. Look in the mirror and you'll see one staring at ya."

Sam shoved Ozzie in the chest. "Screw you, Ossie."

"Who's the poofta now?"

Sam pushed again.

Ozzie didn't back away, but kept his voice quiet. "Touch me again and you're dead."

On the other side of the field, Coach McCulloch saw what was going on and moved to stop it, but Coach Wright put his hand out. "Let 'em work off a little steam. It's gonna happen sooner or later. Better when we're here."

Coach McCulloch wasn't so sure, but he waited.

The cheerleaders stopped practicing and Unity's pom-poms were as still as the afternoon air.

Sam reached out with his finger and held it an inch from Ozzie's chest, toying with him. Just one touch and Sam would win. Either he'd beat this Australian black-and-blue, or the boy would back out of his promise and look like a yellow belly. He looked into Ozzie's eyes, trying to glimpse fear. Sam was taller and heavier, a physical specimen so fine that college recruiters sat up in their fifty-yard-line seats whenever he ran onto the field.

Ozzie never blinked. His shoulders stayed unhunched and his arms hung loosely by his sides. There was a half-smile on his face, like he knew something Sam didn't.

He did.

When Ozzie was ten he had come home from school with a busted lip and a bloody nose—courtesy of three boys who wanted his football—and Pop had taught him how to fight. They'd spent afternoons down at the old dairy, working the heavy bag and speedball, sparring beside a milk vat that hadn't been used since deregulation. After boxing or footy, Pop could gruff out a "not bad" that made Ozzie's heart swell more than a hundred compliments from others. A month or so later Ozzie ran into the three boys again. He got his football back.

Sam moved closer, eyeballing Ozzie, and suddenly a buzz swept around the field. Players, coaches, and cheerleaders shifted their focus from the standoff to a man shuffling across the field.

It was Coach Hayes.

Sam lifted both arms and clapped in Ozzie's face. "BOO!"

Ozzie didn't bat an eyelash.

Sam slowly backed away.

Coach Hayes had hardly seen the Shooters play since the day he retired. He still listened to every game on the radio, but when he showed up in person fans would keep looking at him or asking him what he'd do differently if he was on the sideline, so he stayed away.

His once brown hair was white but still thick like whipped cream, and he looked fit enough to run laps with the players, the way he always had. When Coach Hayes announced his retirement—right after the Shooters beat Denham by a point to win the district title—it turned into a day of mourning that had lasted fifteen years. Some people were angry, saying that the coach had quit because he knew that Denham and their black running backs were soon going to be too good (and they got it partly right because Hope hadn't beaten Denham since), and some were simply grateful for the years of winning he'd brought to Hope. All wanted him back, even when Coach McCulloch went eight and two and made the play-offs in his first season. Coach Hayes didn't just make the play-offs, he won them.

"Hope you don't mind if I visit," Coach Hayes said to Coach McCulloch, as the two men shook hands.

"Not at all."

"Just want to wish y'all luck for the Panther game."

"Sure is kind of you."

His voice got lower, so only Coach McCulloch could hear. "And I want to let you know that even though the dogs are barkin', I think you're doing a mighty fine job, Coach. You can only go with what you got, and by the sounds of it, you ain't got a lot."

Coach McCulloch shrugged.

Coach Hayes hadn't finished. "There's a few people around here, important people, stirring up the pot a little bit. Just want to say watch your back, that's all. And if I can do anything, you let me know."

"Appreciate that."

They shook hands again.

"One more thing," said Coach Hayes. "Do you think I could meet the Australian? Sounds like a real interesting fella."

Coach McCulloch called Ozzie over.

"I knew a few Aussies in Vietnam," said Coach Hayes.

He had no idea who this old bloke was, but Ozzie was impressed. The man actually knew how to pronounce "Aussie."

"Cheeky SOBs," continued Coach Hayes, "but the type of men you'd want beside you in battle."

"My pop was in World War II," said Ozzie. "Spent two years as a POW in Italy. An Italian girl helped him escape. Best time of his life, he reckons."

Coach Hayes laughed. "Sounds like some of the guys I knew." He shook Ozzie's hand. "You keep up the good work out there. And remember, being a Shooter, it means a whole lot to the people who live around here."

Ozzie nodded like he understood, but he didn't. Not yet.

chapter 19

There were three letters waiting for Ozzie when he arrived home from training.

Dear Boofhead,

Hello, mate. Thanks for the postcard. Though next time send one with a picture of Yankeeland on the front. If I want to see my own town I can look out the bloody window.

Good to hear you're doing all right. Mrs. Allan says hello and wants you to behave yourself over there. No playing silly buggers or those Yanks'll chuck you in Guantanamo and throw away the key. And if they don't, Mrs. Allan will give you a good tongue-lashing. I don't know which is worse. Your mate Johnno said to say g'day. He's supposed to be helping me fence right now but he hasn't shown up, the lazy bugger.

The weather is bloody terrible. It's hot and everything is dead or dying. Feed has gone up again. Still, the farm's only something to make the days pass quicker for me now. It doesn't seem long ago that I was a young buck like you, but now I get a shock every time I look in the mirror. A bloody big shock.

You got a letter from the Broncos, I've enclosed it. If they offer you a chance and you're willing to give it a red hot go, then by all means take it. But if you're going to go down there and stuff around, I'd rather you stay here and help me on the farm. God knows I need it. But I've gotten my pound of flesh out of you so you deserve to follow your dream. Just make sure it's the right one. Most times I went to the city as a young fella I ended up in a padded cell. Too many pubs and too many blokes who loved a blue for my own good. But you might be smarter than me. Then again, you may not be.

I've heard you're playing Yankee football. I saw it in the war, bit of a fool's game if you ask me. Too much talking and not enough action. One thing about Yanks is they love to bullshit. They did all right in the war, though, I'll give 'em that.

Well, not much else. Don't reckon I'll play footy this year, wouldn't want to show up the likes of you! Reckon I could still tackle better than Johnno though, the gutless wonder.

Yours truly,
Pop

PS I remembered that try I scored for Queensland. It was at the Brisbane Exhibition Ground and not Lang Park, in 1948. Put that in your pipe and smoke it.

* * * * *

Ozzie picked up the second letter. Unlike his grandfather's this one was typed on thick, official-looking paper, a Brisbane Broncos letterhead at the top.

Dear Austin,

You have been identified by our organization

as being a highly talented junior Rugby League
player. Early next year we are running a
training camp and we'd like to invite you to
participate. It will consist of trial games,
interviews, and fitness and psychological
testing. Some of the players who attend may be
offered a contract with the Broncos, so it is
an exciting opportunity for you.

We are happy to cover your travel expenses for
the camp. Enclosed is some further information.
If you have any questions please contact me.

Best regards,
Cyril Conroy
Brisbane Broncos Development and Recruiting
Manager

* * * * *

The third letter was on pink paper, in neat, flowing writing, with small hearts drawn around the margins.

Hey Sexy,

Thanks for your postcard. Congratulations on making the football team. (Did you have to do anything, like try out!) You and football, it's like you're meant for each other.

I really, really, really miss you! I've been walking around school like a zombie, my friends have been full-on worried and shit. The only good thing is that I'm studying more now that I don't have this hot guy to distract me. (I wonder who that could be?) I even got an A on my last math test! (And I didn't give Mr. Penissi a kiss from you. Though I'd love to see the look on his face if I did.)

Can you believe I've got less than two months of school left? It's blowing my mind. I'm applying to Unis in Brisbane but I could defer and stay around here next year if that's what you want. What do you really want? I know you want to help your pop but you also have to do what's right for you. In the city you could learn a trade and play football. If you really love the farm then stay, but I've never heard you say much about it. Then again, I don't think I've heard you use the word "love" ever, so who knows?

I went around to see your pop and he did a fair bit of bitching about Johnno as per usual. Talking about Johnno, I don't think he's been lifting too many weights, though I saw him lift a heap of stubbies at Jane Frawley's party. He'll never change, that boy. He still thinks you're the bee's knees, of course. He asked about you and I told him to *write and find out. He just laughed. Me and Oz don't need to write is what he said.*

Well, I hope you're thinking and dreaming about me because I can't get you out of my head!
Love ya,
Jess

PS Just because I bought you those postcards doesn't mean you can't write a letter, if you want to, every now and then.
PPS Give me your phone number so I can ring you. And tell me the time difference so I don't wake the family up.

Ozzie wanted to write back straightaway to Pop and Jess, and even to Johnno, to tell him to get his act together. Johnno needed a good kick up the arse every now and then. But there was the game on Friday night and Coach Wright was bugging him to learn the playbook. Plus he had to get up early tomorrow morning and run through some moves with Jose and Mal.

He'd write on the weekend, he decided. For now he'd just look at the photos. Johnno and him lifting the under-sixteen trophy above their heads. A younger Pop with no shirt on, so tanned he was nearly as black as Johnno, sitting on a horse. Jess in her bikini, the day they went swimming in Mitchell's waterhole. The day they kissed for the first time. The photos made him sad and he realized he hadn't really looked at them, or missed home, until now.

He put them away and tried to forget.

chapter 20

On Friday, Sam walked around school with knives in his stomach. When a boy asked, "So you think y'all will win?" Sam didn't even hear the question, let alone answer. He was busy playing the game in his head.

What he saw were passes that kept hitting the open man, just like his dad had taught him. When he was on his game, Sam's passes could hit an open beer bottle, he was so accurate. He could hurl the ball so violently he could smash that beer bottle into slivers of glass.

To Sam's disgust, Coach was practicing more of this crazy offense run by the Australian, but Sam figured if he could get a few good throws in early he could keep Ozzie off the field for at least the first half. Perhaps if he kept throwing well he could keep Ozzie out for the entire game.

While they were reading *The Catcher in the Rye* during English, a message came that Coach McCulloch wanted to see Sam in his office. Walking there, Sam began to fear the worst. Surely a stupid Australian couldn't replace him as starting quarterback? Could he?

"Take a seat," said Coach. "How're you feeling?"

Sam forced a smile. "Ready to go."

"Mmm." Coach paused. "I need to tell you something. About tonight."

The office overlooked the school oval where the cheerleaders were refining their routine for tonight's game. Right now Sam wanted more than anything to look out the window and see Unity, her perfect legs jumping and spinning, her perfect face smiling. *His* girl.

"Want some water?" Coach asked.

Sam shook his head. *How long can I hold onto her if I'm not starting quarterback?* He had another urge to connect with Unity, but resisted. If Coach was going to stab him in the heart he'd make it as hard as possible by looking into his eyes.

"Three big-time college scouts are going to be at the game," Coach said. "One of them is from Justice University." He gave Sam a brief smile. "Just thought that might interest you."

Sam took a deep breath and relief flooded his lungs.

He let himself gaze out the window and he saw Unity being thrown high into the air, her arms spread wide, and it seemed to Sam that Unity hung at her apex for an eternity.

I almost thought things weren't going to be okay, Sam thought. *I almost forgot who I was.*

* * * * *

Under the bright lights of Shooter Stadium there is nowhere to hide, and not too many teenagers can handle the pressure of being the right arm of a team. Sam loved it. Being under the hot lights, people cheering your every move—it made him feel alive. There were nerves, especially tonight against the Porter Panthers, but they were left behind in the locker room.

In the huddle Sam was calm but firm, the way a quarterback should be. "Remember, on pass plays, go straight for their balls when you block. Then the defense'll have their hands down, and our receivers'll have easy catches."

Tex nodded. "It'll be our pleasure."

"Okay, red twenty-seven on two. Red twenty-seven on two." A whistle blew. "Men, we can do this. Follow me and I'll take you all the way tonight. Ready?"

The whole offense yelled, "BREAK!"

The linemen struck at the defenders' groins, which forced their hands down, which meant there were no fingers to deflect Sam's forty-yarder to Malivai (who would also have been doing his best to impress the recruiters except that he didn't know they were watching:

Coach didn't want to make Malivai more nervous than he already was). It was a timing pattern and Sam hit his receiver in full flight, and if Malivai hadn't stumbled after the catch it would have been a sure touchdown.

"Great throw!" yelled Coach from the sideline.

The home crowd cheered and Sam felt good. He could imagine those college boys getting excited, perhaps already reaching for their cell phones, setting up a recruiting visit. This was his night. He felt it. Jose joined them in the huddle, bringing with him Coach McCulloch's instructions: a handoff to Malivai who would run behind Tex's block.

Sam fidgeted with his chinstrap. He wasn't in the mood for a handoff. He wanted to throw again, he wanted another bullet into a pair of hands for a touchdown. "I'm changing the call."

"What?" said Jose.

"Red fourteen on one."

"Another throwing play? But Coach said . . ."

"I don't care," said Sam. "We're about to bust them right open. I can feel it. Come on, men. Red fourteen on one. Ready?"

Tex shook his head.

"Just run the play Coach wants you to," said Jose.

"I'm the quarterback here! Red fourteen on one. Ready?"

A whistle blew. There wasn't time for any more discussion.

"Break." Sam was the only one who said it this time.

Sam play-faked to Jose and dropped back to throw. When he was wired like this everything seemed to unfold in slow motion. He could see his receivers start to run criss-cross routes and knew he could hit any one of them in the chest. He knew, that is, until the Panthers' defense blitzed. It was like someone had hit the fast-forward button, and nine defenders forgot about their opposite numbers and ran at the quarterback like kamikazes. The blitz was a calculated gamble that only worked if the quarterback intended to throw from the pocket.

Shit! Sam thought from the pocket, as he desperately tried to find the room and the time to throw.

Tex stopped one defender with a vicious block and Sam dodged two more who sprinted through so fast they couldn't change direction in time. Sam was just about to let a pass fly when a hand got hold of his black-and-white jersey. He tried to ignore it, pretend it wasn't there, but the hand was strong and it slung him to the ground before he could let go of the ball. Eight bodies jumped on top of him, one for each yard of ground this play had lost, and when he finally rose, Sam was faced with a situation so unusual he couldn't comprehend it.

"Son, you have to go off," one of the referees said to him. "Your coach says so."

"Time-out," said Sam.

"What?" asked the referee.

"Time-out!"

The referee blew his whistle. "Whatever you say."

Sam ran to the sideline. Coach McCulloch grabbed his chinstrap. "First you change the damn call, then you waste a time-out. What in god's name are you doing?"

"I didn't . . . It was an accident," said Sam.

"Well, that's why you're going to the bench. So there'll be no more accidents."

"Please," Sam said, "let me back in. I'll do the job for you, I promise."

There was a hint of desperation in Sam's voice that Coach McCulloch had never heard, that he'd been waiting to hear for three years. Coach thought about doing what Sam asked, but the thought didn't last long. "You run the plays I call," he said. "New quarterback."

The Porter coaches couldn't believe their luck: Hope's quarterback replaced so early in the game! They'd studied the Shooters on screen and knew that they had a talented throwing quarterback and a few good receivers. And that was it. Without their starting quarterback, Hope should be easy pickings.

"I told you our blitz training would pay off!" said the head coach of the Panthers, smiling. "One quarterback down, one to go. We're ready to shoot the Shooters!"

They weren't ready for Ozzie. The Shooters lined up in a formation the Panthers had never seen before, and the Porter defensive captain turned to the coaches on the sideline for guidance. The coaches held their arms out wide as if to say, "You're on your own." But even though they were confused, they weren't overly worried. The Panthers' defense was predicted to be the second best in the district, behind Denham's. But when they saw the Shooters' quarterback take the ball from the line of scrimmage and run, then pass the ball to a receiver as he was being tackled, they started worrying for real. And then when that receiver, after attracting the rest of the defensive team, passed the ball *again*, they started hyperventilating. This wasn't football they were watching. It was freak-ball.

No one touched Malivai as he ran thirty yards for a touchdown, and a recruiter got out his phone. "The Shooters have got a receiver who also plays running back. He's not all that big, but man, can he run!"

Mayor Green and Pastor Slipper were sitting within earshot. "He can sing, too," said the pastor, laughing.

"We might have to hold off on that little project of ours," said the mayor.

The pastor nodded.

The head coach of the Panthers pulled his defense together when they came off the field. The coach's belly jiggled when he talked. "Next time lay off the quarterback! He's gonna pass the ball, so wait until he does, then hit the running back before *he* can pass it. Break him in two!"

Two tackles by Tex and one from Ozzie saw the Panthers kick the ball back to the Shooters. Sam was about to run onto the field, but the coach stopped him. "We'll stick with Austin."

Sam hurled his helmet down.

"We can stick with Austin all game, if that's what you want."

Sam sucked in a breath. "No. I didn't mean . . ."

The coach turned away.

The Shooters lined up in the same formation.

"Snap him like a stick!" yelled the Panthers' coach.

Ozzie took the snap and ran toward Jose, who was taken out by four tacklers. Unfortunately for the Panthers, he didn't have the ball. Ozzie was cradling it in two hands as he sprinted upfield, Malivai in support. By running at the safety, Ozzie made him commit to a player, and at the last second the defender lunged at Malivai and pulled him to the ground. But Malivai didn't have the ball. Ozzie had thrown another fake and a flying dive right under the posts sealed the touchdown.

When the Panthers' defense came off, their head coach screamed at them. "You have to hit the quarterback! Don't assume he's gonna pass the ball, you hear? Don't assume the next guy will pass the ball. Just damn well smash all of 'em!"

But no matter what the Panthers' coach told his players, every time they thought they had a handle on the next play, something would go wrong. It was like this new quarterback had turned the world upside down.

When Coach McCulloch gave Ozzie a well-earned rest, Sam hit Jose for thirty-five yards, then found Malivai for fifty yards and a touchdown. But by that time, late in the fourth quarter, the game was over. The recruiters had moved down to the sideline to meet the standout players, one a running back named Malivai B. Thomas and the other a quarterback who didn't throw a forward pass all night.

When the clock reached ten the crowd started a countdown. As the hooter sounded, cheerleaders and Hopettes stormed onto the field to give the players the hugs of their lives. The band played the school song and the Shooters' supporters stood and sang. They had won, and for the rest of the week there would be a hum around town, and the players could walk the streets like heroes.

Sam sat on the bench rather than celebrate. Unity came up behind him and laid a hand on his shoulder, but he shrugged it off. He didn't feel like a hero tonight, and he didn't need a girl feeling sorry for him. Especially not on a Friday night. Especially not on a football field.

chapter 21

"Let's get messed up!" Tex's voice bounced off the locker-room walls.

The players had showered, drowned themselves in deodorant, and patted on the aftershave that they barely needed. In blue or black jeans with cowboy boots and checkered, button-down shirts, they were ready for the triumphant lap around town in pickup trucks followed by a party at Tex's place. They were waiting for only two players. Malivai was still outside listening to college recruiters whisper sweet promises in his ear, and Ozzie was finishing his first informal press conference.

What did he think of the Hope football program? he'd been asked. *Where did he learn to play like that? Was he a Christian?*

"Austin!" One journalist was waving his hand in the air. "What's the name of that running play?"

"Eh?"

Coach McCulloch spoke up. "We call it 'The Line Formation.'"

"Is that with a capital T?" asked the journalist.

"Yes," the coach said.

"Who came up with the move?"

"Austin and I worked it out together. It's what you call international cooperation."

The reporters laughed.

Ozzie raised his eyebrows. Coach had added a sweeping blocking formation to the play, but the basic idea was his.

"Austin, did your father play football?"

"Nah, but my grandfather was real good. He scored a try for Queensland in 1948."

"Queensland. Is that anywhere near Sydney?"

By the time Malivai and Ozzie were ready, the Hope fans had congregated outside the locker room. They clapped all the players as they stepped out, but they gave The Line Formation boys a hungry cheer.

"Watch out now. Y'all's heads have to fit in helmets next week." Tex grinned at Ozzie, Jose, and Malivai.

Angela pushed forward and slipped a folded-up piece of paper into Ozzie's hand. Once he was sitting in the back of Tex's pickup truck, he pretended to do up his shoelaces so he could read it privately.

Congratulations! U are so awesome! Can't wait to

C U at Tex's tonite. Don't worry about making plans coz I've already told Mr. Graham U won't be coming home till morning. I'll look after U!
Luv Ange
X X X X

Ozzie felt something move down below and it wasn't the truck. Then he thought of Jess. "Girls will want you," she'd said. "Of course I want you to be faithful but that's gonna be up to you."

But what about boys wanting Jess? Some bloke could be hitting on her right now for all Ozzie knew. But then again, she could have had any boy in Yuranigh, and she'd chosen him. "Remember, I'll be waiting when you get back," she'd said.

He scrunched up the note.

* * * * *

One thing Ozzie learned about Americans that night is that they know how to celebrate a win. When Yuranigh made the Grand Final of the South-West Queensland Cup, it was a big deal for the town. In the semifinal they'd trailed their rival, Calamine, right up to the last minute, when Ozzie scored the winning try. For sure, he'd got his share of free beers and pats on the back afterward, but people didn't get *really* excited. They'd

149

nod and shake his hand and the old-timers would say, "You're Jack Freeman's blood all right." A few days later it was mostly back to complaining about the weather and the high tariffs on produce by the Europeans and the Yanks.

Here, teenage boys ran in front of the players' pickup trucks with painted chests and bulging eyes, yelling, "YOU GUYS ROCK!" At Tex's party, girls Ozzie had never seen before hugged him and wouldn't let go. "I love you, Austin," cried one.

Tex unpeeled her and took Ozzie into his bedroom, the only room not jam-packed with people. "It's fun being a hero, hey bro?"

"S'pose."

Tex popped the top off a beer and handed it to Ozzie, and cracked one open for himself.

"Why do they get so excited?" asked Ozzie.

"This is America, man. People love winners."

Ozzie took a swig. "I love beer." He meant it. The first one after a day's work on the farm was liquid gold. It tasted bitter and sweet and made him forget the future and the past, both of which hung over his shoulders like demons. Drinking too much of it was the one thing his father and grandfather had in common. "How do ya stop it going to ya head?"

Tex grinned. "Which one, the fame or the beer?"

"Fame."

"I don't know. Last year we didn't have that problem."

They sat and drank. A poster on the wall listed the ten commandments, but not the Christian ones.

1. The Earth is our Mother, care for Her.
2. Honor all your relations.
3. Open your heart and soul to the Great Spirit.
4. All life is sacred, treat all beings with respect.
5. Take from the Earth what is needed and nothing more.

"Do you know any of those ... Aborigines?" asked Tex.

"My best mate's one," said Ozzie.

Tex took a long swallow. "Not many guys on the team know this, but I'm part Apache."

Ozzie looked more closely at Tex. His skin was chocolate brown but you'd expect that living in this climate. What you didn't expect was an Indian named Tex.

"My ancestors are warriors," said Tex. "Dad says I got their blood."

"Didn't know Indians played footy."

"You know who was named American athlete of the twentieth century?"

Ozzie made his best guess. "Michael Jordan?"

"Jim Thorpe."

"Who's he?"

"The man won himself two gold medals at the

Olympics, then became a pro footballer *and* a baseball star. He's from the Sac and Fox tribe, full-blood," said Tex, pointing to a poster on the other wall.

The man in the picture looked a bit like Tex, only smaller with eyes that were sadder.

"I'm going to head out to the reservation next year, check it out, maybe work the casinos," said Tex.

"What for?"

"Just wanna find out my story, you know?"

They sat for a bit.

"What happened to him?" asked Ozzie.

"Who?"

Ozzie gestured to the man on the wall.

"They took his gold medals off him because he made a few dollars playing baseball before the Olympics. They let him become an American citizen when he was thirty, and by fifty he was a homeless drunk." Tex finished his beer and cracked open another. "Some people found out who he was and cleaned him up, gave him a house. But only 'cause he was Jim Thorpe. Only 'cause he was a winner."

"Better than nothing. In Australia they'd say it was his own bloody fault."

They were quiet again. Ozzie looked back up at the wall.

6. Do what needs to be done for the good of all.

7. Give constant thanks to the Great Spirit for each new day.

8. Follow the rhythms of nature; rise and retire with the sun.

9. Speak the truth, but only of the good in others.

10. Enjoy life's journey, but leave no tracks.

"I can manage 'em all," said Tex, following Ozzie's gaze. "Except number eight. I love to stay up and party."

The bedroom door banged open. "I've been looking for *you* all night." Angela took Ozzie by the arm.

"Watch out, man. That girl's got a reputation and it's not good," said Tex.

As they walked off, Ozzie could hear Tex laughing behind him.

Angela led him to a spot in the backyard. The grass was soft and the desert air was just starting to turn cool.

"Finally," she said, "a chance to really get to know you."

She pulled out a pack of cigarettes and offered him one. He shook his head.

"My parents would die if they saw me now," said Angela. "They're like real conservative, church leaders and everything. Always saying, 'Drugs are evil, Angela.' I'm like, 'I know, Mom.'" Angela took a drag and laughed the smoke out. She took a long gulp from a glass.

"What are you drinking?" asked Ozzie.

"Coke." She took another sip. "With maybe a tiny bit of rum."

Ozzie held out his hand and she passed him the glass. He had a taste. "I'd say there's a tiny bit of Coke with a lot of rum."

She smiled. "Do y'all drink a lot in Australia?"

"Most people do. I usually only have a few."

"Why?"

"Trying to get real fit." Ozzie drank some more beer.

"Football?"

"Yeah. Not the footy you play over here, though."

"Do you want to play in college?"

"Uni? Nah. I might go to the city and play for a club, else I'll stay in Yuranigh and be a farmer."

Angela tapped the ash off the cigarette. "I can't wait to go to college. Mom and Dad want me to go to Mance Christian, which is real strict, with no alcohol and curfews and everything, but I'm trying to talk them into letting me go to Peters, which would be *so* much fun. They have a football team so I could try out for cheerleading and join a sorority and . . . it'd just be awesome."

"Can't you go to whatever uni . . . college you want to?"

"College is real expensive here. I need my parents to pay."

Angela put her hand on Ozzie's arm. "I want to say I'm *so* happy you came to Hope. You know I'm only the second girl to be both a cheerleader and a Hopette, which is *so* neat."

"Who was the first one?" asked Ozzie.

A girl glided across the yard toward them. Angela took her hand off Ozzie's arm. "Speak of the devil," she said.

"Hey, you two," said Unity, sitting down beside them. "Havin' fun?"

"Sure," said Angela.

"Well, I hate to bring bad news, Angela, but Mom just phoned. She said your parents have been trying to get you on your cell all night."

"I turned it off."

"They said you have to be home by eleven."

Ozzie looked at his watch. It was eleven thirty.

Angela threw down her empty glass. Luckily it landed on the grass so it didn't break. "Goddamn it! I'm meant to take Austin home tonight."

Unity raised an eyebrow.

"I mean, back to the Grahams'. "

"I can do that," said Unity. "The Grahams are practically my neighbors. You'd better leave—your dad's freaking out. He said if you're not home by midnight he's comin' to get you."

"I hate living in a small town!" Angela took one last draw from her cigarette and crushed it into the ground. She gave Ozzie a long hug. "We'll do this another time."

chapter 22

Unity opened a beer and passed it to Ozzie.

"You have it," said Ozzie.

"No, I'm done. Got to drive us home."

"I can drive. I've only had a couple."

"You sure?"

"No worries."

"I don't normally drink beer, but . . ." Unity arched her neck and drained most of the bottle.

"Where's Sam?" asked Ozzie.

"Not feeling well."

"He looked all right at the game."

Unity shrugged.

"He doesn't like me much, does he?" said Ozzie.

"I wouldn't say that."

"Come on, I don't mind. He hates my guts, eh?"

Unity paused. "I guess he does."

"Why?"

"Tonight he spent most of the game on the bench, watching someone else be the hero."

"No one's a hero in footy. If the team wins it's all good."

"Some people don't see it that way."

"Do you?"

"Do I what?"

Ozzie looked at her. "Do you have to be the best?"

Unity brushed back her thick hair. "I'd like to say I don't care. But I guess I do."

Ozzie lay back on the grass. The moon was hiding for the moment and the stars shone like fireflies. There was no Southern Cross but the sky looked almost the same as it did from the other side of the world.

"You were great out there tonight," said Unity.

"I didn't know what I was doin'. Got lucky."

"It didn't look like it. You're so calm. I'd be scared to death."

"I feel the same watchin' you. You did the splits and my groin started hurtin'."

She smiled. "Surprised you noticed. Aren't you supposed to be concentrating on the game?"

Ozzie looked at the moon, which was now giving him a quarter-smile. "Can't concentrate all night."

There was a pause. "I know Sam gets scared," said Unity. "He just doesn't admit it."

"I get scared, too. I'm just good at not thinking about it."

157

Unity lay back beside him. "Tell me about Australia."

"It's a lot like here. Just different."

"How?"

"Well . . ." He thought for a second. "Lots of little things. Like, we don't wear pads to play footy, for one thing."

"Do y'all tackle?"

Ozzie smiled. "Sure do."

"Then how can you not wear pads? Don't y'all get hurt?"

"Sometimes. But we don't really worry about it."

"Why not?"

"Dunno. S'pose there's a lot of stuff that can hurt you in Australia."

"Like what?"

"Snakes, for one thing. Greenies are all right, but black and brown ones, they can kill ya."

"I hate snakes."

It was quiet, until Ozzie slithered a finger across Unity's belly. "Ssss," he said.

"Aahhh!" She punched his shoulder. "Don't do that!"

"Come on," said Ozzie, getting up. "I can't wait to drive on the right side of the road."

"You always drive on the wrong side?"

"Very funny."

Ozzie opened the front left door. In Australia it would

have been the passenger's door, but here it was the driver's side. "This should be interesting," he said.

"You have your license, don't you?" asked Unity.

"Been driving since I was six." He started the VW convertible and threw it into reverse. The gears crunched. He'd actually put it into fourth. "Sorry."

He tried again and this time it worked. Changing gears with his right hand felt weird, like the time he broke his wrist and had to do everything, such as cleaning his teeth and wiping his backside, with the wrong hand. He crunched the gears again and winced.

Unity put some music on—country. Something about drought, drinking, and divorce.

"I love this music," said Ozzie.

"Me, too."

"It makes you happy to be alive." He tried not to smile but couldn't help it.

"Now who's the funny one?" she said.

Ozzie gave the car some more juice and it responded. "Is this your mum's car?"

"My sixteenth birthday present."

He shook his head. "Hell. I think I got a kick up the arse for my sixteenth."

"I'm an only child so my parents spoil me. You have brothers and sisters?"

"None that I know of."

Unity looked at him. "Is that a joke?"

"Nah. Mom died when I was eight and Dad left. Haven't spoken to him, so he could have a few kids by now, for all I know."

"I can't imagine . . ."

A pause.

"Why'd your dad leave?"

Ozzie didn't answer.

"I'm sorry, I shouldn't have asked."

"No, it's all right," he said. "It's just that, I don't really know. He didn't want to be a farmer so he and Mum opened this café in town. Dad cooked and Mum ran the business side of things. It was doing okay, too, till Mum died. Dad tried to keep it going but . . . You have KFC over here?"

Unity smiled. "If we drove north we'd be in Kentucky tomorrow."

Ozzie smiled, too. "Yeah, stupid question. Anyway, KFC opened up in Yuranigh and everyone started going there. Cheap food and quick; it was the place to hang out. Still is, for the kids and that. Dad blamed KFC when his place went downhill, but he was drinking a fair bit and didn't know much about the books, so who can say for sure?"

"Did he meet someone?"

"Nah, just took off. Left a note and said he'd ring once he got himself set up. I was nine then. Still hasn't rung, the bastard."

Unity rested her hand on Ozzie's leg. "I'm sorry."

"Nah. It was years ago. I'm doing all right. Pop took me in and got me playing footy and here I am."

"Here you are."

Except for the country music, they drove in silence.

"Next left," said Unity. "I want to show you something."

It was a dirt road and Ozzie resisted the temptation to do donuts. She stopped him in the middle of nowhere.

"You don't have an ax in the boot, do ya?" said Ozzie.

Unity laughed. "How would an ax fit in someone's shoe?"

Ozzie laughed, too. "Not your shoe, in the back of the car. The boot."

"It's called the trunk."

"A trunk is an elephant's nose."

They got out. Unity opened the trunk.

"What are you doing?" asked Ozzie.

"Getting an ax from the boot."

Instead, she held up a beer and a vodka cruiser. "We gotta drink these before I get home."

"Don't tell me, your parents would kill you if they found them."

"No, they'd kill *you* after I told them you put them there."

Unity led him to a ladder and they climbed and climbed. At the top of the water tower they opened their drinks and looked down over West Texas. Trucks and cars made a dotted white snake along the interstate. The lights of Denham, though farther away, shone more brightly than the lights of Hope. Past that was the blackness of the desert.

"I love it up here." Unity lay back and looked at the sky.

"Yeah. It sure is purdy," said Ozzie.

"Look who's picking up the lingo?"

"Too right."

"Two what?"

"Don't worry."

Unity rolled on her side and took a drink. Ozzie could feel her eyes on him.

"Tell me about your hometown," said Unity.

"Nothin' to tell."

"You're not getting out of it that easy. One story, that's all I ask for."

"Okay." Ozzie thought for a bit. "I can't think of any."

"Come on. What's something your town's famous for?"

Ozzie thought again. He took a drink for courage. He wasn't a natural storyteller, but his grandfather had told this one so many times that he almost knew it by heart. "Okay, here goes. There're plenty of big properties where I live. Pop's place is two thousand acres and that's small, tiny, compared to some."

"Wow."

Ozzie looked at her. "You takin' the piss?"

"What?"

"You know. Makin' fun of me?"

"No. Now hurry up!"

"All right." Ozzie paused, trying to remember where he was up to. "Anyway, in the old days there was this bloke working on a real big property, mustering cattle. Something like a million acres. And there were so many cows that the bloke realized that even if a thousand head went missing, the owner wouldn't know. So he decides to steal 'em. Trouble was, he couldn't sell them in Queensland or New South Wales, 'cause the cows were branded and people'd know. So he drove them all the way to South Australia, right through the middle of the desert."

"Drove them? In a truck?"

Ozzie laughed. "No. On horseback. I'm talking years ago."

"Was it far?"

"Bloody far. There's these famous explorers, Burke and Wills, who died trying the same thing. And this fella wants to do it on his own with a thousand cows."

"What happened?"

"Well, the bugger made it. He sold the cattle, but the owner of the station missed his prize white bull and realized what was going on. The bloke got arrested and brought back to Yuranigh."

"Did they hang him?"

"Let me finish and I'll tell ya."

Unity slapped his arm.

Ozzie gave her a look but kept going. "Everyone knew he was guilty. There were witnesses and everything. But the jury was real impressed with what the bloke had done. He'd survived in the desert, so he was a real bushman and that means a lot where I'm from. So when the judge asked for a verdict, the jury guy said, 'Not guilty' and the judge said, 'What?' 'Not guilty,' said the jury guy again, and the judge said, 'Well, better you than me.' The bloke walked away scot-free."

"I like that story," Unity said.

"Apparently I'm related to the bloke who stole the cattle. Pop says he's my great-great uncle or somethin'. "

She wriggled closer. "I knew you'd be interesting, once you actually said something."

"Oh, thanks."

She laughed. "No, I mean you don't talk about yourself much. Not like the guys around here. With them it's all me, me, me."

"I've got to live with *me* all day. Why would I want to talk about him?"

Unity rested her head on Ozzie's thigh. "Do you mind?"

"Nah." And he meant it. His powers of resistance were severely depleted.

"You and Jose seem close," she said.

"He's a good bloke. Same with Mal and Tex."

"I love Malivai. And Jose." She smiled. "I love Tex, too."

"You tell Sam that?"

"I don't tell Sam everything."

Ozzie couldn't stand it any longer. He placed his hand in her hair and lightly stroked, all the way down to her neck. Unity looked up at him and smiled, and goosebumps invaded his arms and legs. It wasn't cold but he shivered, and the beer in his bladder suddenly screamed to be let out. Somehow this girl was so perfect that his mind and body rebelled.

"We should get home," he said.

"I'm just getting comfortable."

Ozzie could see her open lips, soft and full, and wanted more than anything to hook them between his and not let go.

"We'd better," he said.

Climbing off the water tower was the last thing he felt like doing, but Ozzie scurried down like he was being chased.

Once hooked, you could spend your whole life chasing a dream like Unity.

SECOND
HALF

★

chapter 23

At the Friday morning pep rally, the teachers wore black and white, the band played "Deep in the Heart of Texas," and cheerleaders sprang cartwheels down the gym floor, showing off their underwear. Everything was the same as last week except for the mood—which was more upbeat than it had been in years—and the seating arrangement. This week Ozzie was moved to the front row.

"Ladies and gentlemen," said Principal Fraser. "Before I call Coach McCulloch up here to address y'all, I thought I'd let our newest star say a few words. I just want to say how lucky we are to have an athlete of his ability at Hope, and I guess it shows that our international recruiting scheme is starting to pay dividends."

Mr. Fraser paused for laughter, but there was none. The students probably thought he was serious. "Anyway, here he is. Austin Eaton!"

The students whistled and cheered like they had for Sam at "The Beginning," and Ozzie broke into a sweat. Angela had mentioned something about this but he thought she was joking. He'd been up at the front of school assemblies before, nearly always to collect a sports award, but he'd never had to say anything.

Ozzie took a breath, got out of his seat, and wandered over to the microphone. On the way Mr. Fraser pumped his hand.

"Yeah, thanks for all that," he began, surprised at the sound of his own voice through the speakers. "I'd just like to thank everyone for being here today . . . although this is school so you probably don't have a choice, eh?"

A few people laughed. Mr. Fraser wasn't one of them.

"Yeah, well, umm, I want to say that I'm havin' a good time here in America. The team's real good and, umm, everything's goin' . . . real good. I hope we can score a couple of tries, umm, I mean touchdowns tonight. That'd be good. Yeah, thanks."

He walked back to his seat wondering if that was the worst speech of all time, but everyone was clapping so he didn't feel too bad.

"The Mickson Bulls are big and tough and they're gonna be comin' after us. But our boys are ready." Coach McCulloch pointed at the players, sitting tall in their seats. "They know that one good game doesn't make a season, and tonight's a chance to get y'all excited about

Hope football again." The coach spread his arms wide, as if embracing the entire student body. "But we need y'all to help out. If you can do your part, I've got a feeling tonight'll be something special. This is your team, the Hope Shooters!"

He sure knew how to pump up a bunch of kids. The male students—football players, soccer players, cowboys and musicians—started making animal noises.

"So, you think y'all will win?" a boy asked Ozzie after the rally.

"Dunno, mate. Whadda you reckon?"

"Sorry?"

"Me name's Ozzie, anyway." He put out his hand.

"Excuse me?" said the boy, shaking a hand and his head. The other quarterback always ignored him, but this one didn't speak American. The boy wasn't sure who he liked less.

* * * * *

There were fourteen thousand people at Mickson Stadium that night, and among the crowd were eighteen reporters, here to see the innovative new offense that the Shooters were running. The last one to squeeze into the press box was a small man with a slightly crooked goatee, whose looks belied his reputation as a football scribe.

"Well, blow me down if it's not *the* Chip Paskell," said

Brent Sherlock, the *Hope Times* sports reporter. "Must be a slow news night in Dallas."

Chip grinned. "Just passing through and thought I'd catch a ballgame."

"No one passes through this part of the country unless they're running from love or the law." A few journalists chuckled. "Admit it, you're in West Texas to see how football should be played. Hard."

"I'm sorry, are the Armadillos playing tonight?"

The fourteen reporters who weren't from Hope laughed. "Ooohh," said Brent. "That's a low blow. Laugh all you want, men, but this just might be Hope's year."

The reporters took Brent's advice. For the next few seconds they laughed all they wanted to.

"I'm not here to see Hope win," said Chip. "I just want to see a crocodile hunter play quarterback. Now *there's* a story."

A few reporters raised their pens in agreement.

Down on the field, Coach McCulloch started with Sam as quarterback and kept him in for the whole first quarter. The reporters became restless.

At training that week the Shooters coaches had never seen Sam work harder. Instead of complaining about the linemen who couldn't protect him or the receivers who couldn't catch his passes, he shut up and did what he was told.

"This boy might make a soldier yet," Coach Wright had said.

"Sam doesn't give a damn about the team," Coach McCulloch replied. "He's doing it for himself. But I don't really care, as long as it works."

It *was* working. Sam hit Jose on a comeback pattern and Malivai on a down and in. At the end of the quarter Sam had already made considerable gains. The trouble was that only one pass was caught in the end zone, after the double-teaming of Jose and Malivai left Billy-Joe Powers open to score the first (and probably only) touchdown of his career.

With the score locked at 7–7 in the second quarter, Coach McCulloch put The Line Formation into action. Now that other teams had seen and studied it, the coach was nervous as to how it would go. After the first play he got even more nervous when the Bulls' backfield blitzed and hit Ozzie for a five-yard loss.

Most reporters in the press box guffawed as Ozzie was driven into the synthetic grass and piled on by half the defense. "Welcome to America," said Chip Paskell. He'd driven 250 miles to see what the fuss was all about, and now the Australian couldn't even make it past the line of scrimmage.

On the next play he got enough material for an entire story.

A Change for the Better
by Chip Paskell

In the wide-open spaces of West Texas, life unfolds more

like a book than a movie. Whether it's words, crossing
the main street, or change, nothing much happens
in a hurry. The Hope Shooters football team has won
over 200 games running the same offense for 30 years.
That's what you call tradition. But this year, when head
coach Ben McCulloch knew his team lacked the size to
compete, traditions were broken and change rolled in
like a thunderstorm.

An Australian thunderstorm named Austin Eaton—
exchange student and expert rugby player. He and Coach
McCulloch have invented a new style of offense called
The Line Formation, and if all this sounds strange, that's
because it is.

In Friday night's game against the well-regarded Mickson
Bulls, the Shooters scored one of the finest touchdowns
that this reporter has ever seen. It was simple yet brilliant,
and in order to understand it you need to forget everything
you thought you knew about football.

Eaton got the ball and immediately lateraled it left, to
Jose Garcia. Then, instead of blocking for Garcia, Eaton
ran behind him, receiving the ball back from a short
pass. Eaton faked another pass back to Garcia (you'd be
excused for thinking they were playing basketball) and
cut through a hole opened up by a block from Tex

Powell, one of the few big men in the Shooters' lineup. Eaton scooted over twenty yards, but rather than be content with the first down he lateraled the ball again, this time to star receiver Malivai Thomas, who scored without a hand being laid on his black-and-white jersey.

The brilliance of The Line Formation is in using the no-limit backward pass rule to its full effect. You think the above touchdown was a fluke? Then you should have witnessed the three more scored that night.

"It's something that came to me on a hot, sleepless night," said Coach McCulloch, describing a style of offense that may revolutionize football in this country. "I got together with Austin and talked it through and it's working real fine."

Real fine, indeed. According to Coach Stewart of the Mickson Bulls, "After that first touchdown I started getting nervous. By the end of the game I had ulcers. Unless you break the Australian's leg, I think it's near impossible to defend against this Lion (sic) Formation."

Coach McCulloch isn't convinced that's true. "We'll keep refining it but I'm sure the defenses will keep adjusting. We're just going to take it one game at a time."

One of those games will be against the Denham
Armadillos, currently ranked the number one high school
team in Texas and third best in the country. If The
Line Formation can get Hope its first win against the
Armadillos in fifteen years, then it, and Coach McCulloch,
are definitely for real.

Before the story was published, Chip e-mailed a copy
to the *Hope Times*.

```
To: Brent Sherlock
Subject: My most humble apologies
Message: I still think Denham will kick your
butts.
```

A few minutes later Chip received a reply.

```
To: Chip Paskell
Subject: Apology accepted
Message: A chicken fried steak you're wrong.
```

chapter 24

Angela cut and pasted the story into a leather-bound scrapbook with *AUSTIN* painted on the spine, which almost completed her weekly duties as a Hopette. Last night she'd baked Ozzie a special batch of brownies, plus made a sign to celebrate his Most Valuable Player award. She'd done this rather than attend the postgame party at Curtis's place, although it wasn't her choice not to go. After last week's bash, her parents had been waiting when she'd arrived home.

"Angela, are you all right?" Her mom had peered into her eyes and panicked when she saw how red they were. "Oh my goodness, don't tell me my little girl has been drinking!" She put her nose near her daughter's shirt. "And I can smell . . . smoke!"

Mr. Janus grabbed his daughter's shoulders. "Did any boy take advantage of you?"

Tears welled up in Angela's eyes. "I'm fine, Daddy."

"Angela?" said Mrs. Janus. "We need to hear what happened."

Angela started quietly sobbing. "Okay, there *were* alcohol and cigarettes at the party. But I didn't touch either. I actually tried to get people to stop, that's why my clothes smell."

"Is that the truth?" asked Mrs. Janus.

Angela started crying more vigorously. "I can't believe you'd even ask me that!" She looked at her father. "I swear on the Bible, Daddy."

Mr. Janus took her in his arms. "Of course we believe you, pumpkin. And we're proud you tried to be a good, Christian influence on the other kids. But no more parties with alcohol. There's an old saying, 'If you dance with the devil, he's gonna do the leading.'"

Fresh from an early night, Angela spent Saturday morning making herself beautiful. It wasn't a difficult job. Lots of people were saying that she had a good chance of being crowned homecoming queen later in the year.

Once she was finally ready she kissed her mom and dad. "I have to go visit Austin."

"You seem to really like this boy," her mom said.

Angela held her arm. "Mom, he's becoming so popular. I'd love to show him around. Maybe I could borrow your car?"

"What's wrong with yours?"

Angela screwed up her face.

"If you want the Beamer," her dad piped up, "he'd better be a Christian."

"We were talking about God just the other night."

"We'll think about it, dear," said Mrs. Janus. "Have fun."

"But not too much fun," said Mr. Janus.

Angela waited till she was behind the wheel before she rolled her eyes at her dad's comment, and waited till she had turned out of her street before she lit her first cigarette of the day.

* * * * *

There was a knock on the door and Ozzie put down his pen. All he'd written so far was "Dear Jess." He'd promised himself he'd get this letter finished and posted today, but the morning had been taken up eating (pancakes, eggs over easy, and hash browns) and endlessly replaying last night's victory with Dave. Then he'd shot some baskets with David Jr. and after that Alison had some friends over for lunch. They'd giggled and talked to Ozzie for ages and even asked him to sign their stomachs, which was pretty embarrassing. But they insisted, so he did it.

"You have a visitor," said Nancy.

Angela appeared, a short cream skirt emphasizing her long brown legs, her crop top revealing a stomach tightened by gymnastics and hours on the latest abdominal machine. A beaming smile lit up the red, white, and blue on her face—not the American flag but lipstick, eye-shadow, and medically whitened teeth (which wouldn't turn yellow even if you smoked). Ozzie had noticed that American girls (and boys, for that matter) took their looks a whole lot more seriously than the Aussies did. Heck, Jess would chuck on an old pair of jeans and a T-shirt and be ready to go to the movies. Here, girls dressed up to go to *school*.

Nancy shut the bedroom door after Angela. "I'll give y'all some privacy."

"What's up?" asked Angela, sitting on the bed.

Ozzie put the letter in a drawer. "Not much."

"For you." She gave him the brownies.

He tapped his stomach. "You're making me fat, you know."

"There's a sign as well; it's in the front yard."

Ozzie looked out the window, and above a wooden stake stuck in the turf was a large drawing of a player wearing number twenty-two—Ozzie's number. He was running with the ball and the letters MVP were above his head, with lots of other messages and drawings that he couldn't make out because his bedroom was on the second floor.

"Geez," said Ozzie. "People'll think I love meself."

Angela looked down.

"You okay?" said Ozzie.

She didn't say anything.

"What is it?"

"Well . . . I spent all last night making you cookies and a sign and you don't even say thank you."

Ozzie grimaced. "Oh, sorry, Ange. It's just that . . . I'm not used to all this. Where I'm from people don't give you squat-diddly."

Angela looked up. She stared at Ozzie with puppy-dog eyes.

"So . . . thank you," he said. "For the great sign and the unbelievable bikkies." He pulled one out and took a bite.

"Can I at least have a hug?" said Angela.

Ozzie moved over to the bed and wrapped his arms around her. He was still chewing. Her breasts pressed against his chest until, after what seemed like hours, she leaned back and looked into his eyes, her left hand behind his head, her right stroking his neck. He took a last swallow of brownie.

Angela didn't move, not one inch, but waited. He was resisting, or at least trying to, but she was a stunner and his body took control of his mind.

Ozzie kissed her, like she knew he would. Her eyes were closed but she led him, at first soft and slow with barely parted lips, and then wider and deeper.

And then she stopped. "I don't normally kiss on the first date."

"Is this a date?" He was already feeling guilty, probably because he wanted to keep going.

She got up and brushed down her skirt. "You know, in America we say 'diddly-squat.'"

They both laughed.

Ozzie felt better, then. But only until he pulled out the letter to Jess after Angela had gone. He couldn't think of one thing to write.

* * * * *

That night the phone rang. Angela had said she'd call, so Ozzie wasn't surprised when Alison brought it to him.

"G'day, stranger."

It shocked him. Not only because of who it was but the accent—so exaggerated it was like she was putting it on.

"Hi, Jess."

There was a pause and they both went to say something. International phone calls only allow one voice at a time, which is not how nervous lovers talk. Jess finally got the rhythm of the conversation back on track. "So how ya goin'?"

"Good," said Ozzie. "You?"

"All right. Missing you, though."

"Yeah."

He thought of something to say. "How'd you get my number?"

"From your *letter*."

It took Ozzie about a second to realize he was in

trouble. In these situations he always found it best to say nothing.

"What's going on, Ozzie? You got a girl over there?"

Ozzie couldn't believe she'd just asked him that. He could still smell Angela's perfume on his shirt.

"It's just that, well, you haven't written for weeks."

"Yeah, sorry." It felt like he'd spent half the day apologizing to girls. "Look, Jess, things have been crazy over here, with footy and stuff. But I've been thinking about ya. I was writing you a letter, right when you called."

"Pull the other one."

"No, I was. Really."

"All right, read it."

"What?"

"Read the letter."

"Well, it's not finished."

"Read what you've got so far."

"But that'll spoil the surprise."

"Read it or I'm goin'."

He knew she meant it. "Hang on." Ozzie picked it up.

"Dear Jess." He cleared his throat.

"Go on."

"Umm. Hello."

"Wow. Great letter."

"Hang on, give me a go. Thanks for your last letter. It was really, umm, good."

"I'm gonna go."

"No, don't, Jess. Look, I said I was sorry. Can't we just have a talk?"

"Maybe later. Write your pop a postcard, he's worried about you. So was I."

"Jess . . ."

"Bye, Ozzie."

There was a click, and almost straightaway the phone rang again. Ozzie answered, hoping it was her.

"Hey, stranger."

"Angela . . ." It was a different "her."

"I had fun today."

"Yeah."

"Guess what? I told my parents I have this special friend from Australia and they said I could borrow Mom's BMW and spend the whole day with him."

"Do I know the bloke?" Ozzie wanted to say no, but he didn't know how. Besides, getting away from Hope, forgetting who he was, it was just what he felt like.

"There's one condition, though," said Angela.

"What?"

"You have to come to church in the morning."

"What?"

"Church. It'll be fine, everyone's real friendly. And it'll give Mom and Dad a chance to meet you."

Ozzie didn't say anything. The last time he'd been in a church was for his mom's funeral.

"Are you okay?" asked Angela.

"Do I have to do anything? Like, pray or somethin'?"

Angela laughed. "You don't have to do anything you don't want to. I'll be sitting beside you the whole time. Trust me."

"Mmm."

"I'll pick you up at eight forty-five," she said. "Wear something nice and bring a change of clothes for later. Pack your swimming trunks as well."

"Righty-o."

"Oh, and bring your passport, just in case."

"In case what?"

"You'll see."

Ozzie got one more call that night. He was beginning to feel like he knew why his grandfather never wanted a phone.

"How're you feeling, boy?" It was Coach McCulloch.

"Yeah, good."

"Look, things are bound to get a little crazy around here, especially if we keep winning. You don't worry about what they say in the papers or on TV. Just stay focused, you hear?"

"I'll try."

"See you bright and early, Monday. I want you to show me a few more of those rugby plays."

"Rugby League."

"What?"

Ozzie couldn't be bothered. "See you later."

"Bye."

Before he had time to talk himself out of it, Ozzie dialed Jess's number. Australia was fifteen hours ahead so it was already tomorrow in Yuranigh, and maybe things would be different tomorrow.

But he never found out. An Australian would say Jess was engaged, but in this case Ozzie preferred the American version. Her line was busy.

chapter 25

At eight forty on Sunday morning Ozzie came downstairs dressed in an RM Williams button-up shirt and his very best pair of pants—fraying, coffee-stained blue jeans. Nancy took one look at him and gently suggested that he change into something more churchlike, but the next best thing Ozzie owned was a footy tracksuit.

After foraging in their wardrobe, Nancy brought out a suit that Dave still had from college, when his stomach hadn't yet expanded from too many pecan pies. It was very 1980s but would have to do, and Nancy was still tying the thin black tie (Ozzie didn't know how to do it) when Angela rang the doorbell.

"Well, look at you!" said Angela.

Look at you, thought Ozzie.

She wore a strapless black dress, a red jacket that covered her shoulders, and more makeup than you could shake a stick at. Gold dripped from her ears and a matching necklace hung to her cleavage. On the end of the necklace was a gold cross. Her hair was loose, shining down her back.

Ozzie's eyes widened.

"Shall we?" said Angela.

"What?"

"Go."

Ozzie shook his head. "Yeah, course."

At the front of the church was an electronic billboard that flashed, "Hope Shooters 40, Mickson Bulls 28. Thank you, Jesus!"

They drove into an oval of asphalt almost as big as a football field. An usher directed them, and so many BMWs dotted the parking lot that by the time he got to the front door Ozzie would have been hard-pressed to find the car he had arrived in. If it wasn't a Beamer it was probably a Lexus, a Volvo, or a good ol' American Cadillac. It seemed God looked after His own real well, here.

Inside, rows of seats were filled with smiling women in long dresses, kids who pulled and tugged at their Sunday best, and men with bowl-like haircuts that were short but not too short. Ozzie's scruffy curls were as out of place as a Muslim headscarf.

They arrived at a pew near the front where Angela's family was sitting. Once introduced, Mrs. Janus gave Ozzie a hug, while Angela's little brother gave him a cheeky grin, like he knew the real reason Ozzie was at church. Mr. Janus gripped Ozzie's hand like he was trying to break it. "So this is the boy my little girl's been talking about?" He looked at Angela. "He could do with a haircut."

"Dad!"

Mr. Janus gave Ozzie a tight-lipped smile. "I'm sorry. But if I don't look out for my beautiful girl, who will? I'm a little protective when it comes to Angela, because I was a boy once and I know how young men think."

"Dad!"

"There I go again. Let's change the subject. Tell me, Austin, do you own a gun?"

Ozzie wasn't sure what to say. His grandfather had an old .22 that Ozzie had used often enough, but it wasn't his. "No."

Mr. Janus looked disappointed. "I got my first gun when I was eight. Still love to hunt."

"What do you shoot?"

"Deer mostly, a few quail, and boys who treat my daughter wrong."

"Dad!" said Angela.

Ozzie went quiet.

The service started, and in the introduction Pastor Slipper drew attention to the fact that "this morning we are blessed with the attendance of Hope's newest football star and Friday night's MVP." Ozzie even had to stand up. He felt like a fool, and when he sat back down he wanted to slink even lower and crawl out the door.

Angela took off her jacket and spread it over their laps, slipping her right hand underneath and resting it on his leg. This made him feel better until he remembered that Angela was sitting beside her father.

Pastor Slipper put his hands in the air. "We are here today to give thanks to the one, true, Christian God, a God who sent his only son, the Lord Jesus Christ, to die for each and every one of us. This is a God who wants us to be rewarded both now and in the eternal life after our deaths. To receive this reward, all we need to do is accept Jesus as our personal savior and ask that our sins be forgiven. That's all we have to do, and we will have riches beyond our wildest dreams."

"Seems easy," Ozzie whispered to Angela.

She gave his leg a squeeze.

The pastor kept praying. "And so we are here to confess our sins to God, and if there's anyone in this room, anyone at all, who hasn't yet accepted Jesus Christ as his or her personal savior . . ."

Ozzie could have sworn that Pastor Slipper was looking right at him.

". . . then we pray with all our hearts for that person. For if one sheep is lost, we must help it be found."

"AMEN!" answered the congregation, so loudly that Ozzie jumped in his seat.

Then there was music. Well, not at first, just a large choir clapping a beat. There was no organ, no guitar, and none of the wind instruments that Ozzie had grown accustomed to from the school band. But when a boy stepped forward and started singing, eyes closed and hands clenched into fists, there was definitely music.

> *People get ready, there's a train comin'*
> *You don't need no baggage, you just get on board*
> *All you need is faith to hear the diesels hummin'*
> *You don't need no ticket, you just thank the Lord.*

The choir started humming in the background.

> *People get ready, there's a train to Jordan*
> *Picking up passengers coast to coast*
> *Faith is the key, open the doors and board them*
> *There's hope for all among those loved the most.*

For a few seconds Ozzie shut his eyes. He forgot about his girlfriend in Australia; he forgot about football. The voice washed through him and made everything clean.

> *People get ready, there's a train comin'*
> *You don't need no baggage, just get on board*
> *All you need is faith to hear the diesels hummin'*
> *You don't need no ticket, just thank the Lord.*

The voice stopped.

"Holy hell, can he sing or what?" Ozzie said to Angela.

"Shhh," someone hissed from behind.

Pastor Slipper stood and began walking around, a microphone clipped to his collar. "People of God, I want to talk to you about something that's been troubling me. Yesterday I turned on the TV, not late at night or in the early hours of the morning, but at seven thirty p.m.— family time—and let me tell you what I saw. There was a man and a woman, and they were having . . . sex."

Ozzie stifled a laugh. People around sucked the roofs of their mouths, making *tch* sounds.

"Now in the show this man and woman weren't married. In fact, they hardly knew each other. But it didn't stop them engaging in what Paul himself declared *the* most holy, sacred act of God."

A couple of people murmured "Amen."

"And let me tell you something that troubled me even more. These two characters showed no guilt or remorse, and imagine the message that sends to the young men and women who watched television at seven thirty last night across America."

"Amen." It was a little louder this time.

"I know a lot of people might say, 'Big deal. This is the new millennium. Loosen up a little bit, Pastor.'"

A few chuckles.

"But if Americans can't see that fornication and

homosexuality and sexual deviancy are ruining our country, then God knows, this ain't the country I grew up in!"

"AMEN!"

The pastor was working the crowd now, getting them excited.

"The America I know is not a country that accepts boys and girls as young as ten experimenting with drugs and sex. The America I know does not admit that the union of two unmarried people before God is anything less than a grave sin. And those who commit that sin without begging and praying for God's forgiveness will do no less than BURN in the fires of hell!"

"AMEN!" Angela joined in with everyone else.

The rhythm of the pastor's voice became faster and more urgent. "The America I know is a country where men are men and women are women. Heck, I walked down the main street of Denham the other day and saw two men with tight shirts and hair in, what are they called, ponytails? And two women, both wearing pants, with hair so short you could hardly tell it was there. This ain't what God wants for our country, people! He wants an America where a family means a husband, wife, and well-behaved, God-fearing children!"

"AMEN!"

"You remember what God did to Sodom and Gomorrah when they started sinnin' in a disgusting way? He sent down an army of angels and those towns EXPLODED in a fire that could never be put out. And don't you believe, people, that He couldn't do the same thing to America. And when He does, He will start in Hollywood—and take out all the fornicators and gays and deviants—and leave the God-fearin' people of West Texas, the good, Christian families like yours and mine, alone."

"AAAA-MEN!"

Angela's hand slipped out from under her jacket. "Amen," she said, smiling at Ozzie.

Ozzie leaned back and saw a statue of Jesus on the cross, at the front of the church, frowning down on His people.

chapter 26

After church Ozzie wasn't too keen on another discussion with Angela's dad, so he excused himself and had a look around. There were arches and domes made of marble, and Ozzie was examining a stained-glass window with an intricate drawing of an apple tree when someone tapped him on the shoulder.

"I didn't expect to see *you* here," said Malivai.

"I didn't expect to hear *you* sing like a bloody pop star," said Ozzie.

They laughed and shook hands.

"So what'd you think?" asked Malivai.

"About church?"

"Yep."

"Good music."

Malivai smiled.

"It feels a bit strange, though," added Ozzie. "I don't

really fit in, you know?"

"Join the club," said Malivai.

"Yeah, not too many people look like you, eh?"

"Most blacks go to church on the south side, where Reverend King has a choir that sings so high the notes almost reach heaven. This congregation is what you'd call more"—he leaned in closer—"musically challenged."

"They've got good cars, though," said Ozzie.

"They sure do."

"Do you have a good car?"

He shook his head. "We have an old Buick that barely starts."

"Then what are you doing here?" Ozzie joked.

Malivai shrugged. "When I was a boy my parents moved to an apartment north of the interstate."

"That must be all right."

"It's so close that when the oil tankers drive by our windows rattle like in an earthquake. If we'd stayed on the south side we'd own a house by now, but even with Mom and Dad working we can barely afford the rent."

"Why'd they move?"

"For me. My parents are always talking about breaking the cycle."

"What cycle?"

"Poverty and ignorance." Malivai touched the stained-glass window. "Live in a place that's drug and crime free, get a college education and a good job, and the cycle's broken. That's my dream."

"You have a hundred universities almost breaking down your door," said Ozzie. "You'll break the cycle, no worries."

Malivai didn't answer.

"C'mon," said Ozzie. "Everyone thinks you're a legend."

Malivai shrugged. "The white people are friendly enough. But if I couldn't sing, or run, maybe to them I'd just be another nigger. And at school, when I walk past the brothers from the south side, sometimes I think they're waiting for me to slip up."

"Hey, you two."

Ozzie turned and felt his stomach drop. "G'day, Unity." He hadn't seen her in church. There were so many people, though, that it wasn't surprising.

"You gettin' some tips on how to sing?" Unity asked Ozzie.

"No way."

She touched Malivai on the shoulder. "He's good, isn't he?"

"Real good."

She smiled and looked at Ozzie. "I didn't know you were a Christian."

Ozzie could see Jesus on the cross, behind Unity. He also spotted Angela approaching. "Me neither."

Angela put her arms around Ozzie. "Unity Summer-Andrews. Stop trying to steal my man."

197

Unity looked at Angela like she was joking, but that look changed when Angela gave Ozzie a kiss.

"Wow. That happened quick," Unity said.

"Too quick," added Malivai, grinning.

As Ozzie walked out the huge oak church doors, he turned and looked back. Unity was standing close to Malivai, and there was something about the way Mal looked at her that Ozzie recognized.

It was desire, of wanting something you can't have.

* * * * *

Once on the interstate Angela set the cruise control for 70 miles per hour, only slowing when the high-pitched beeping of the radar detector told her to. Seventy in the Beamer felt smoother than sixty in Pop's pickup, and that was when it was traveling at 60 *kilometers* per hour.

Ozzie jumped in the back to change into jeans and a T-shirt, so he wouldn't wreck Dave's suit, and saw Angela peeking at him in the rearview mirror.

"So, where're we going?" he asked.

"Guess."

"Give me a hint."

"Think history class."

"The Alamo?"

"Farther south."

"South America?"

"Not that far."

"Do they speak a different language?"

"*Si.*"

They were there in less than two hours, which wasn't nearly as far away as Ozzie thought another country would be. At the border Angela gave a man $20 and drove over a bridge. Going the other way, from Mexico to America, Ozzie could see cars lined up for miles, with customs officials checking under seats for drugs and in trunks for illegal Mexicans. From America to Mexico there was no line and no one bothered checking anything. Angela and Ozzie could have brought in a carload of illegal Americans, but it seemed that no one cared.

Once they drove over the bridge and past the sign that said *¡Bienvenidos a México!*, everything looked different. A few hundred meters back were fast-food joints, a shopping mall, and a freeway. Here, there were food stalls, narrow cobblestone streets, and a strange smell.

Angela parked and gave a boy some money to watch the car. They walked down an alley lined with clothes stalls, shoe stalls, and beggars. People were calling out to them in a language Ozzie didn't understand, and Angela began talking to an old woman at one of the stalls. At first the conversation seemed friendly enough, but then it became heated. Angela pulled Ozzie away but the woman called out urgently, and they turned and went back. The woman handed Ozzie some Levi jeans.

"Try 'em on," Angela said. "If they fit, they're yours."

They fit. Ozzie started unbuttoning them (these jeans didn't even have a zipper) but Angela told him to leave them on. She handed a wad of bills to the woman.

"How much were they?" Ozzie asked as they walked away.

"Fifteen dollars," said Angela. "Could've had 'em for ten but I felt sorry for her."

Ozzie realized that Angela had nothing in her hands except a handbag. "Where are my jeans?"

"I gave them away."

"What?" Ozzie and his jeans had shared a lot of history.

Angela put a hand on his shoulder. "Just think, some Mexican boy is probably wearing them right now. And I'm sure he needs them a lot more than you."

Ozzie's makeover was just getting started. Angela bought him three brand-name T-shirts, a pair of loafers, and a Dallas Cowboys cap—all for under $20. Ozzie had mixed feelings about his new look. He felt semicool, but he was sad that Angela gave away his poo-brown T-shirt and his Dunlop Volleys (which once were white but now were the same color as the shirt). "Just one more thing and you'll be perfect," said Angela.

"No way," said Ozzie, as they stood outside a barber's shop. "I'm like that Samson bloke—my hair gives me strength."

"I love your hair," said Angela, ruffling it with her fingers. "But if you get it cut my dad will like you more, which means he'll let you take me out on Friday nights, which means . . ." She put a hand around the small of his back.

"No," said Ozzie.

"Just a trim," said Angela, moving her hand down lower and squeezing.

Ten minutes later the hair that curled down over Ozzie's neck and ears was chopped off. Part of him would be staying in Mexico forever.

Angela looked at Ozzie approvingly. "That's enough work for one day. Time for fun."

She took him to a bar where they leaned back in bamboo lounge chairs. "You know, in the States," said Angela, "you can die for your country at eighteen, but you can't buy a drink until you're twenty-one."

"How old do you have to be here?"

"Old enough to afford it." A waiter came past. "*Dos Coronas, por favor.*"

"What'd you just ask for?" said Ozzie.

"Two beers."

In the corner a man was cradling his guitar like a baby and plucked out songs that made Ozzie feel homesick, even though he'd never heard music like it before. After they'd listened for a few drinks, not saying much at all, Angela gave the waiter $2 and he handed her a key.

"Follow me," she told Ozzie. She took him to a room

that had a double bed, a sink, a box of tissues, and a spider crawling across the ceiling.

Angela sat on the bed. "I want to thank you for today. For coming to church and meeting my family. I'm sure it wasn't easy for you."

"Your dad's pretty scary."

She smiled. "I know."

"Does he mean that stuff, about shooting boys who like you too much?"

"Sure. But what he doesn't know won't hurt him."

She patted the sheet and Ozzie sat next to her on the bed.

"Can I tell you something?" said Angela.

"Yep."

"That night at Tex's party, I was worried you'd hook up with Unity."

"She's got a boyfriend."

"That doesn't matter."

"Why not?"

"'Cause now you're the best player on the team"—she took his hand—"everybody wants you." She placed his hand on her breast. "I want to make sure you only want me."

They fell back onto the bed, joined at the mouth, and Ozzie's legs felt light—like they weren't connected to his torso.

"Have you got . . . something?" Angela asked a little while later.

It took Ozzie a moment to realize what she meant. "No."

"You're lucky I come prepared." She reached for her handbag.

Ozzie hesitated. "I haven't . . ."

"What?"

"You know."

"No way!"

Ozzie looked away.

She giggled. "It's okay, I promise to be gentle."

This wasn't how Ozzie imagined his first time. On a bed in Mexico with a girl he didn't really know or understand. He'd wanted it to be with Jess, but on the night before he went away she'd stopped him at the critical moment. "You need a reason to come home," she'd whispered.

But when Angela unbuttoned her shirt and Ozzie traced his tongue up her brown stomach until it came to the whiteness of her breast, he felt weak. His body rocked up and down and something dropped on his back and stung him, though he hardly felt it. Nothing meant anything until he'd proven his manhood and did what he was put on earth to do.

But then, afterward, the wanting and the weakness were gone and he loved Jess and Pop and Rugby League. Angela slept, but Ozzie's eyes were open, looking at the dead body beside him. The eight legs of the spider were curled up tight.

chapter 27

Ozzie jumped at the chance when Angela asked if he wanted to drive home. He'd never been in a car this good before, let alone driven one. It'd be something he could tell his mates. He turned her on and she purred like a kitten. With just a finger on the wheel she did exactly what she was told.

If only girls were as easy to handle.

Angela sang. Ozzie could tell that she thought she was pretty good. She used expression in her voice, emphasized the same syllables as the pop star on the radio, but it didn't really help because Angela couldn't sing to save herself. Ozzie didn't say anything, though. It was funny, he thought, you could share the most intimate experience with somebody, but it didn't mean you could be honest with them.

The rhythm of driving helped Ozzie reflect on the day.

He was eighteen, away for half a year, surely he'd done what any bloke would have? So why did he have this worm crawling around in his gut?

Until recently, he could always look Jess in the eye and tell her the truth, no matter what he'd done. But what if she asked about today? What would he say?

It was just part of the whole experience, eh? You know, making new friends, understanding other cultures, sharing bodily fluids. I'm not a bastard like my dad.

Maybe it would be easier, for Jess's sake, if he just denied it. Just to stop her getting hurt.

Maybe the worm in his gut was from the shots of tequila he'd had before they left?

Suddenly, a police car did a screeching U-turn and the siren screamed. They were still a mile from the Mexican border. Ozzie pulled over.

"Shit," said Angela.

The policeman tapped on the driver's window with two big smiles—both his mouth and his mustache turned up at the sides. "You made a bad turn, mister."

Ozzie wasn't in the mood for fools. "That's impossible, mate. This is a completely straight road."

"Shoosh!" said Angela, but it was too late.

"Please step out of the car, mister."

"Me?" said Ozzie.

The policeman glanced at the backseat and then back at Ozzie like he was stupid.

Ozzie had to put his hands on the roof and spread his legs. The cop patted him down—touching places Ozzie preferred he didn't—and then took the wallet out of his pocket. "I check for drugs," he said.

The policeman also took Angela's wallet and sat in the police car for a long time, looking through them, leaving Ozzie standing in the hot sun with sweat trickling down the inside of his new jeans. The policeman came back. "I need for you to follow me to the station, so I can write you a ticket."

"Do you think we could just pay for the ticket now?" said Angela.

The policeman looked at the sky. "I think that could be arranged."

"How much?" asked Angela.

"Two hundred dollars. U.S."

Angela took a sharp breath. "I don't have that much."

The policeman smiled. "Perhaps Mr. Australia can lend you some money."

Ozzie didn't tell the cop that Australia was where he was from, not his name.

"Okay, then," said Angela. "But we need some money for gas. How about 150?"

The policeman looked at the sky again. "I take 180."

He took $150 out of Ozzie's wallet and the rest from

Angela's, who knew never to bring much money into Mexico.

"Can I get back in the car now?" asked Ozzie.

"Let me give you one piece of advice." The policeman smiled again. "In this country, if the law says you made a bad turn, you made a bad turn. *Comprende*?"

Ozzie said nothing, just got back in the car. He and Angela were quiet until they were over the border.

"I didn't think you had much money," she said.

"I get paid to play footy. I usually give it all to my granddad, but a few months ago we made the Grand Final and that was my bonus. I s'pose that bloke needed it more than me."

They smiled.

"You can see why us Americans have no sympathy for countries like that," said Angela. "They deserve everything they damn well get."

Ozzie handed Angela his wallet. "Can you put this in my backpack?" He didn't want it flogged by any more police.

She reached inside the bag. "There's food in here. Can I have it?"

"No worries."

She peeled off the wrapping and took a bite. "It's good."

"What is it?" Ozzie couldn't believe there was anything tasty in his backpack.

"Some kind of chocolate." She read the label. "Caramello ko-waaa-laaa?"

"What?"

"Caramello ko—. Oh, I'm eating a koala bear? Sorry, Mr. Koala, but you taste too good." She put the rest in her mouth and Ozzie suddenly remembered.

A card and a Caramello Koala to help you fly.

The chocolate was a present from Jess.

Thirty minutes from Hope they stopped at Denham and went to the pool. Even though it was late afternoon the Texas sun was still strong, and Angela lay on the grass and had Ozzie rub tanning oil into her brown skin.

There was no high diving board like the one at Yuranigh Public Pool (for insurance reasons), but Ozzie joined the line of little kids and did front flips off the low board. He was having a great time until he noticed a bloke lying next to Angela, talking intently. He did one more dive, lifted himself out of the pool and wandered over.

"G'day."

The boy ignored Ozzie. "You should visit more often. Some of us miss you round here." He put his hand on Angela's arm.

Ozzie moved closer and dripped some water on the bloke's head. That got his attention. "Well, if it isn't the big shot from Australia?" he said, standing up. He was a fair size, and though Ozzie had taken down bigger, when some other boys came over and two of them were almost as big as Tex, Ozzie decided he'd rather not start anything with the guy's mates around.

The boy continued. "Let me make it real easy for you, with the language difference and all." He stepped closer. "Shit-kickers who play for the Shooters don't come to Denham and steal our women. They just don't."

One of the mates chuckled.

Ozzie wasn't sure what this bloke was on about, but he didn't like his tone. "I don't want to steal anything," he said. "I just want to piss in your pool."

The bloke spat tobacco at the ground and some of it landed on Ozzie's big toe.

"Stop it!" Angela said to the boy.

Ozzie counted silently. It was something Pop had taught him. Pop always said that it's all right to punch a bloke, but only if you still feel like doing it after you've counted to ten. At eight he still wanted to, but one of the mates spoke.

"What are we gonna do, man? Kick his ass?"

"No. We'll let him go, 'cause of Angela." The boy looked at Ozzie. "But next time we see you, we're gonna bust your head clean open. Game or no game."

"We're number one. Hope can't hide and they sure can't run," said the mate.

"You make a good cheerleader, buddy," said Ozzie.

One by one the boys spat in the direction of Ozzie's feet, then walked away.

"Nice blokes," Ozzie said to Angela.

"I used to go to school here," she said. "The guy talking to me was my old boyfriend; he plays for the Armadillos. The other guys are on the team as well."

"When do we play them?"

"Six weeks."

"Can't wait."

Ozzie dived into the pool and washed his feet clean.

chapter 28

Five more games, five more wins, and the Hope Shooters had football fans in the entire state of Texas talking. "The surprise package of the season," said texasfootball.net. "A renewed coach and new offense have led the Shooters into territory unfamiliar since the legendary Coach Butch Hayes was at the helm. Their only hiccup for the big game against the Armadillos could be a suspect shoulder for star lineman Tex Powell."

At their last game Hope had scored forty-two points against the Range Glory and more than half had come from traditional football plays, with Sam throwing the ball like his future depended on it. Afterward, a representative from the renowned Justice University promised to organize a visit and Sam could hardly wait. Perhaps college was a place where he could be number one again. The stand-alone quarterback, not this sharing crap where the other guy got all the kudos.

Although The Line Formation had been effective, Ozzie and Coach McCulloch both thought that against Denham they'd need a fourth player to provide more options. The defenses were starting to catch on, and there were only so many tricks Ozzie had up his sleeve with two support players. Ozzie asked for Billy-Joe Powers, but Coach had someone else in mind.

"You can't be serious?" Sam Wilson said when Coach McCulloch told him.

"I've never been more serious in my life. We're up against a team with the number one defense in the country. We need something that's gonna shake 'em up."

Sam's head slumped forward.

On Monday, while the other players were running stairs, Sam was taking directions from Ozzie. "You hold the ball in two hands, lift your right elbow, and sort of flick it with your wrists. Like this." Ozzie passed the ball to Jose, who returned it with exactly the same technique.

"I'd rather pitch it, like this," said Sam. He palmed the ball in his left hand and flicked it sidearm to Malivai.

Ozzie looked doubtful. "I don't think it's as good. You can't dummy, I mean, fake, as easily. Just try it this way, okay, mate?" Ozzie passed him the ball.

Sam pitched it back to Ozzie, his way. "I'm not your mate."

"Fine." Ozzie passed to Sam, hitting him in the chest so hard it knocked the wind out of him. "Okay, wanker?"

"I'm gonna find out what that means," said Sam. "And if it's what I think, I'm gonna kick your ass." He pitched the ball at Ozzie's head.

Ozzie ducked.

"C'mon guys," said Malivai. "Stop swingin' your dicks and start practicing. I'm gettin' cold."

You'd think Sam would have caught on easily. He was a coordinated athlete who'd grown up with a football in his hands. The trouble was this wasn't the football his dad had taught him, and perhaps it was his subconscious that wouldn't let his body obey. At first he had trouble learning how to throw in the underhand style of a Rugby League player, then he couldn't catch the pass on the run ("I ain't no receiver") and then he couldn't run *and* pass.

By Wednesday morning everyone was getting frustrated, including Ozzie. "Mate, just try!" he said, after Sam had lobbed a pass behind Jose's back.

Sam snatched up the ball and threw it between the goalposts, forty yards away, American-style. "That's what happens when I try."

Malivai went to run after it.

"Don't," said Ozzie. "Let him get it."

Sam didn't move.

"Get it," said Ozzie, taking a single step closer to Sam.

Sam bumped Ozzie on his way past, but instead of getting the ball he walked right past it.

* * * * *

Later that day, when Sam closed the door on the young woman taped up inside his school locker, another stunning young woman was there in front of him. Except this one wasn't wearing a red bikini, and she wasn't smiling.

"I heard you walked out of practice," said Unity.

Sam shrugged. "I wouldn't call *that* practice."

She glared at him.

"Who told you, anyway?" asked Sam.

"Austin."

"Why do you even talk to that asshole?"

Unity raised her voice and a few nearby students turned their heads to listen. "That 'asshole' is helping us win. It seems that everyone appreciates it 'cept you."

Sam shook his head. "I threw three touchdown passes last week. What do the papers write about? The Ossie and his goddamned trick play."

Unity moved closer. Her expression softened. "You have a chance to do something real special for this town. We can beat Denham! But right now you're screwing it up, just because it's not all about you. Keep that up and you might lose more than a game."

She walked away.

During history, Unity sat next to Ozzie. While they watched a DVD on the Civil War, learning how 618,000 people died for no good reason (which gave Ozzie a whole new perspective on "state versus state, mate versus mate"), Unity leaned over and whispered, "How are things going with Angela?"

Ozzie wasn't sure what she meant, so he didn't answer.

"Is she looking after you real fine?"

"Yep."

"That's good. She's a sweet gal."

Ozzie nodded. He could smell perfume, and if there ever was a sweet girl it was the one sitting beside him.

"I just want to warn you about something," said Unity. "You know Angela used to go to Denham?"

"Yep."

"Well, just watch what you say to her, because she's still friends with some of the players and—"

"She wouldn't do that."

Unity touched his arm. "Look, I'm not saying anything, it's just . . . there's a lot riding on this game. I know she still sees the guy she used to date, and . . . you can never be too careful."

"Unity!" came Miss Webb's voice from the back of the room. "Stop talking football and watch the war!"

Ozzie looked up to see a Confederate soldier get stabbed with a bayonet.

* * * * *

After the pounding of hard-work Wednesday, Coach McCulloch called Sam into his office. "Someone wants to talk to you," he said, before he shut the door and left.

Sitting at the desk was Coach Hayes. He had a pen in his hand. "How're you doing, Sam?"

"Fine, sir."

"Coach McCulloch asked for me to visit. Is it okay if we talk awhile?"

Coach Hayes had a way of asking a question that had only one possible answer.

"Yes, sir."

Coach twirled the pen around his thumb. He saw Sam watching. "Instead of listening in school I spent too much time doing this." He spun the pen again and put it on the desk.

"You know, Sam, I saw your daddy play once. I was in North Texas, visiting, and I watched a college game. Your daddy was the quarterback."

Sam blinked.

"I remember one play like it was yesterday. A receiver ran a fly pattern and your daddy hit him in the hands from fifty yards. It was some throw."

Sam felt a surge of pride.

"Let me tell you something else. The best quarterback I ever had, he couldn't throw a lick compared with your daddy."

Sam frowned. He didn't trust quarterbacks who couldn't throw. "He must have been fast."

Coach smiled. "He could run but not that fast. Five seconds flat for the forty."

"Then why was he so good?"

"That boy understood what football was all about, the same thing that made this country great."

Coach paused.

"What?"

"It's simple. But just because it's simple doesn't mean it's easy. If it was, everyone would be doing it. Everyone would be a winner." Coach picked up the pen. "If I called a running play, that boy would hand off to the fullback and block for him like a boy twice his size. Put his body on the line every time if I asked him to. He didn't care how we got into the end zone or what play we ran, just as long as we did. And at the end of the game he'd be bloody and tired and sore, but he could look at himself in the mirror, win or lose, and be proud."

Coach looked into Sam's eyes. 'That's all I ask of you, Sam. If you can look inside yourself and know you've done your best, not for yourself but for your team, then you're a winner. In my book, in America's, and in God's.

That's all there is to it. I'm an old man now and I have no regrets, but there's only one thing I'd like to do if I could go back in time. And that's play football. That feeling of everyone being together, individual cogs all working to make one, well-oiled machine, having teammates I'd lay down and die for, and knowing they'd do the same for me. I'll never get over that feeling as long as I live. I just hope there's football in heaven. That's all I hope."

Sam left the office and Coach Hayes twirled the pen. The speech had come back to him like blowing a whistle, which is hardly surprising seeing that he had given it hundreds, no, thousands, of times. He hoped this would be the last.

The pen fell from his fingers and landed on the floor and the coach didn't try and bend down to get it. He felt old. He'd watched a dozen presidents come and go, he'd been in a real war, a cold war, and a war on terror, and he'd lived through the innocent, rebellious, and greedy years. He didn't trust his body anymore and he wasn't sure whether he trusted the creed of sacrifice that he'd dedicated his life to following, in the nation, and notion, that was America.

chapter 29

The week prior to the Shooters/Armadillos game was always a tense one for the towns of Hope and Denham. Even if your house straddled the border, it was impossible to sit on the fence and support both teams, or you'd be treated as a double agent. In the diner where Ozzie, Angela, Unity, Sam, Jose, Tex, and Malivai sat, the window sills were painted black and white, and streamers hung from the ceiling. You wouldn't find many Denham supporters drinking coffee here.

The students were waiting for a photo shoot. In years past the mayors of Hope and Denham had a longstanding bet about the game, which involved the losing mayor having to wear the winning team's jersey for a week. After the fights over district lines and twelve straight wins for Denham, Mayor Green put an end to that tradition. This year, however, with a district championship on the line, it was revived. And so the *Hope Times* and the *Denham Statesman* had organized a photo opportunity for the two mayors, so they could smile and shake hands while wearing high-school football jerseys that barely covered their fat stomachs, surrounded by players and cheerleaders from both towns.

But the mayors were late. Their respective personal assistants kept phoning, asking if the other mayor had arrived yet, and when the reporters said no, each mayor suddenly had to attend to urgent matters of local government.

"Man, those guys are big," said Jose, looking through the window at the Denham players.

"They're not *that* big," said Tex.

Ozzie had to agree with Jose. They were huge. He recognized a few of them from the pool and he couldn't help but remember what they promised to do next time they saw him. He decided to change the subject. "Did they get their trophy back yet?"

Unity shook her head. "Their principal is freaking out. Apparently, the glass in the cabinet wasn't even broken."

"Which makes it an inside job," said Jose.

Six pairs of eyes were trained on Angela. She smiled. "Why y'all looking at me?"

"You did go to school there . . ." said Malivai.

"And have friends who own a master key," said Unity.

"I hope you use it as a toilet," Sam said.

Tex laughed.

Angela gave a little smile. "As I told Mr. Fraser, I'm happy to take a lie detector test."

"I've read that those things can be beaten," said Jose. "But only by professionals."

"Angela's a pro all right," said Sam. "Just ask Austin."

Tex laughed.

"Sam!" Unity punched her boyfriend.

Ozzie thought it was time for another subject change. "Who started this stuff between the schools?"

"Denham," said Tex. "They suck."

Unity elaborated. "On Sunday night five armadillos were let go inside our cafeteria."

Ozzie squinted.

"Animals, not players," she said.

"Oh," said Ozzie.

The group chuckled and Unity continued. "Then some Hope students set off firecrackers on their playground, which caused a huge panic."

"Why?" asked Ozzie.

"Two words, my Australian friend." Tex held his thumb and pointer finger in the shape of a gun. "School shooting."

"The easiest way to become famous in this country is to walk into a crowded room with a gun." Jose shook his head. "It's the American dream gone wrong."

"I'll tell you my American dream," said Tex. "Find the pricks who painted the Armadillos' logo on our locker-room wall."

"Yeah, that was nasty," said Malivai. "Two nights ago, wasn't it?"

"Yep," answered Unity. "But stealing the district trophy from Denham is even nastier."

Everyone looked at Angela again.

"Stop it!"

"Does this happen every year?" asked Ozzie.

"Not this bad," said Unity.

"That's because this time we've actually got a chance," said Jose.

"We've got more than a chance," said Tex. "We're gonna knock 'em on their asses."

"Is your shoulder okay?" Angela asked Tex.

Tex shrugged. "Nothing a needle won't fix."

Malivai put a hand on Tex's shoulder. "You might be the new 'Shrimp.'"

Everyone, except for Ozzie, chuckled.

"Shrimp was this great Shooters' running back who broke his leg in the Armadillo game," Jose explained. "He not only kept playing but went on to score three touchdowns. It was years ago, but in Hope, he's still the man."

"Hasn't paid for a beer since," said Tex. "I'd take his place, any day."

"'Cept you'll be called 'Whale,'" said Malivai.

Tex tried to cuff him around the head but Malivai ducked out of the way.

The teenagers were called outside. The mayors had finally arrived, after the reporters had told both of them that the other had shown up.

"Their cheerleaders are cute," said Sam, as they walked out.

Unity hit him. "They're not *that* cute."

The Hope and Denham players were introduced to each other by the respective mayors. After giving his ex-girlfriend a hug, the Denham captain squeezed Ozzie's hand so hard that it started throbbing. "What I said before will happen at the game," he said. "And that's a promise."

The other Armadillos smirked.

* * * * *

At the Friday morning pep rally the band played louder, the cheerleaders jumped higher, and the students yelled longer than they had all year. The first thing Coach McCulloch did was to ask for the stolen trophy to be placed outside his office sometime over the weekend. "There'll be no questions asked," he said. "We need it safe because we want to be drinking out of that thang next week."

Despite his piss-poor effort last time, Ozzie was called out front to address the school. He looked at his shoes when he talked. "Hello. Umm, tonight's an important game, and if we win it'd be, umm, real good."

Ozzie wondered what he was doing there, when for some reason he raised his head and looked into the crowd. People were hanging on his every word. It was like everything he said had a deeper meaning, like everything he said was true. He stood up straight and kept looking, into eyes that wanted to see, and Ozzie himself started to believe.

"When I left Australia I wasn't sure what to expect, but I sure wasn't expecting this. It's like . . . I love Australia, but Hope, it's real good, and America, it's real good, too, and . . . I'm not sure I want to go home."

Some kids laughed but most nodded their heads.

"No matter what happens tonight, I promise to do my best, because I love playing football for this team. I know that all the blokes, I mean, guys, love playing for the school and for the whole town. We're all fired up and we'd like nothing more than to bring y'all a victory tonight!"

Ozzie raised his arms when he said the last bit and the students stood and clapped and stamped their feet.

Unity hugged him first, then Angela, and even Sam shook Ozzie's hand as he made his way back to his seat.

"Well said, man," said Sam. "Well said."

* * * * *

Hope to Choose Homecoming Queen

By Lydia Sales
TIMES Education Writer

Four excited girls are nominees for this year's homecoming queen. Unity Summer-Andrews, Angela Janus, Leesa Gray, and Braidie Reilly make up the Queen's Court, and the winner will be crowned during half-time at the Shooters versus Denham football game.

Summer-Andrews is favored to win, but a few experienced observers say that newcomer Janus might spring a surprise. "I think the judges will be impressed by her openness," said a former queen, Nancy Graham. "She's an active member of the church and a delightful young lady."

According to Janus, "Winning's not everything. Of course I'd love to win, but it's an honor just to be nominated. I just can't wait for the homecoming dance!"

Most students feel the same way, and the Hope High gymnasium is expected to be rocking on Saturday night to the sounds of local band

Good Habits. Prizes will be awarded for the best costumes.

The Hope homecoming celebrations have a long tradition stretching back to the early 1900s. It was seen as a weekend for men who left small towns seeking work to "come home." Many former Shooters football stars will return to Hope to watch the game, including Chad Barnes and Tim "Shrimp" Ward.

chapter 30

Before the game, trainers taped ankles, coaches tapped laptop keyboards, and Malivai was joined by a surprising number of teammates in the bathroom, emptying their guts. No one said much until fifteen minutes before kick-off, when Coach McCulloch called the team into a huddle.

"I don't know about y'all, but I've been waiting for this day for a long time," Coach said. "Ever since I got here, all I've heard is Armadillos this and Armadillos that, and I'm sick of it. This year we're as good as them, and don't any of you not believe it."

"Yes, sir," said a few of the players.

"I don't need to tell you that this is a game you'll remember for the rest of your lives. Now, *how* you remember it is gonna be up to you. It'll either be something you look back on with pride, or something you'll try your damn hardest to forget."

Coach paused for a few seconds. "If every link of the chain is strong, it can't be broken." He paused again. "If every link of the chain is strong, it can't be broken." He pointed to the boys.

"If every link of the chain is strong, it can't be broken!" they chorused.

"AGAIN!"

"IF EVERY LINK OF THE CHAIN IS STRONG, IT CAN'T BE BROKEN!"

"Yes." Coach spoke more quietly. "Yes. Don't just say it. Do it!" He picked at a scab on his arm. "Captains?"

Tex went first. "Let's work our asses off out there. No matter how tired we are, how much we're hurting, let's keep going until either they kill us or we kill them. For this one night, let's have no excuses."

Malivai spoke softly. "I've been hearing that it's impossible to score against these guys. That their defense is too strong. Well, I'm gonna score. I don't care if I have to run around the whole team to do it. Defense, keep them under twenty points and I promise the offense will do its job."

"Sam?" asked Coach McCulloch.

Sam stood, a football in hand. He was about to say something but stopped.

"We don't have a whole lot of time," said Coach.

Then Sam did something no one expected. He threw an underarm pass, Rugby League–style, to Ozzie.

The whole team shifted their gaze to Ozzie as he

clutched the ball. He didn't say anything, just bit his bottom lip and stared at the ceiling.

"Austin?" said Coach, looking at his watch.

Ozzie looked at the team. "Just remember, fellas. It's only a bloody game." He threw an overarm pass back to Sam.

* * * * *

This is it, folks, what we've all been waiting for. Twenty thousand people crammed into Shooter Stadium about to find out the one thing they came for—who's gonna have bragging rights for 365 long Texas days.

With forty seconds left to play, Coach McCulloch has called his last time-out, so let's recap what's happened so far.

The Denham Armadillos have been ahead all game, but the Shooters have refused to go away. Denham scored first with a five-yard sweep and the Shooters hit back with an incredible fifty-yard touchdown by Malivai Thomas, the ball passing through six sets of hands before Sam Wilson delivered the final lateral in a new-look Line Formation. A crossing pattern got Bobby Blake over the line for Denham and it looked as though they might blow the game wide open, but back came the Shooters with a thirty-five-yard touchdown pass by Wilson into the waiting arms of Jose Garcia. The Armadillos were knocking on the door all third quarter but only came away with a field goal, and now it's Hope's chance to steal the ball game.

The Shooters have the ball on their own ten-yard line, so ninety yards stands between glory and grief, but it's going to take a miracle with no Austin Eaton. He was knocked unconscious when three defensive linemen speared him headfirst into the ground in a sickening tackle. Whether or not it was deliberate is impossible to say, but don't be surprised if Hope supporters don't forget or forgive for a very long time. So, with the score 17–14 to the Armadillos, the players are coming back onto the field, and both sets of fans rise to cheer on their boys for one last do-or-die drive.

The players take position, Wilson in the shotgun. He gets the snap and drops back into the pocket. Denham defense breaks through! Wilson throws hurriedly and it's . . . complete! Thomas pulls in a high ball and steps out of bounds on the 21. First down, Shooters.

Listen to that Shooter crowd. They haven't given up yet, though this will be the comeback of the century if Hope can pull it off.

Hurry up offense, Wilson in the shotgun, here's the snap. Wilson fakes to his running back and throws. Garcia has it! He's at the thirty, forty, he's gotta get out of bounds to stop the clock. He does! Garcia makes it all the way to the forty-five before taking it out with nineteen seconds remaining. Oh my Lord, this is getting hard to watch!

Look at those Armadillo coaches yellin'. They sure ain't happy with their all-star defense, but two great passes under pressure by Sam Wilson have lit this game right up.

Shooters in the huddle. The offense clap hands and they're out. There's the snap and Wilson rolls right. Throws long for Thomas who's double-teamed. Could be an interception! Thomas jumps, and . . . brings it down at the Denham twenty-yard line! First down, Shooters, but the clock's still ticking. Wilson sprints to the line. Nine, eight, seven . . . they might not get another play! Linemen in position, but what's this? Thomas still hasn't gotten up. The referee blows his whistle with . . . two seconds on the clock! Whoa, that was close.

So one more play. The Denham fans aren't happy with the injury time-out, I'm sure you can hear it for yourself. I've been watching Malivai Thomas play football for three years and have never seen him fake an injury. Come to think of it, I've never seen him get an injury, he's always been too fast. They're bringing out the stretcher as we take a look at the instant replay and . . . oh dear, it looks nasty. His knee twisted and buckled underneath him when he landed.

Surely Hope will send their field-goal team in now to tie up the game. No! It looks like they're going for the win! One play to go, a touchdown needed. And what's this? Austin Eaton has run onto the field! Out like a light in the second quarter, he's back from the dead and in the quarterbacking position! Wilson is to his right in The Line Formation, then Garcia and then Billy-Joe Powers.

Here's the snap. Eaton laterals the ball to Wilson, who runs and fakes a lateral to Garcia. Wilson turns inside and laterals back to Eaton, who's got some space on the left.

Eaton's not running! Oh my God, what's happening! Defense converges and . . . Eaton throws! Eaton throws! He throws forward to Wilson, who catches the ball on the ten, now at the five . . . TOUCHDOWN, SHOOTERS! Someone's taught this Aussie kid to throw like an American and it's won a town a championship. Oh my Lord, I've never seen anything like it! Eaton and Wilson are hugging. Fans are bursting onto the field and pandemonium has broken out. They're starting to tear down the goalposts and it's ugly but beautiful at the same time . . .

Coach Hayes switched off the radio, drank his last mouthful of antacid, and smiled. Wilson and the Australian working together to bring a famous victory for Hope? Who would have thought it possible?

Maybe, just maybe, he'd underestimated today's America. Maybe it wasn't so bad after all.

* * * * *

Three Shooters were carried off the field that night.

One was Sam, who'd always dreamed of this, although in his dream it was different. In it he threw a touchdown-winning pass, raised his arms in the air, and was carried off by his dad.

Instead, his dad was trapped up east on business. Jay Wilson had arranged for his ex-wife to send a tape of the game, but only if the Shooters won.

Sam had caught a wobbly pass on a trick play by an Australian, a play that Sam had worked out that very morning as they ran through their last practice of The Line Formation. "What if Austin learns how to pass?" he'd said.

"I know how to pass," said Ozzie.

"No, I mean *really* pass."

Malivai and Jose nodded. "They wouldn't know what hit 'em," Jose had said.

And so in ten minutes Sam had taught Ozzie how to throw the pigskin—to spread his fingers over the laces and flick his wrist and get a spiral humming.

In many ways Ozzie was the real hero, Sam knew that. Ozzie had got that pass away with linemen bearing down like a pack of wolves who'd already knocked him out once and now wanted to finish the job. All Sam had done was catch the ball and run ten yards into the end zone without tripping over grass.

This wasn't what Sam had dreamed, not at all.

It was better.

Suddenly, Sam asked to be put down. There was something he needed to do. "Where is she?" he yelled.

"Who?" someone asked.

"The homecoming queen."

From out of the crowd she appeared, and Sam said something that he couldn't remember saying and meaning before in his life.

"I'm sorry."

"What?"

"I'm sorry," repeated Sam. "I've been an asshole."

"Say it again."

"I'm an asshole."

"No, the other part."

He put a hand out. "I'm sorry."

It was only then that Unity went to him.

Ozzie was carried off as well, though he knew he wouldn't remember much, even as it happened. A fog was spreading through his mind now that his body had done its job. He'd been concussed before and it wasn't the worst thing in the world. Sometimes it even gave you more, rather than less, clarity. You saw inside yourself and you weren't scared anymore. Maybe that's why it was so dangerous. Once you stop being scared on a football field you're asking for trouble. Before he'd come to in the dressing room—courtesy of smelling salts from the doc—he'd had a sense that he almost knew who he was and what he wanted out of this strange journey called life. He wanted to stay there, actually, but the doc was clapping and Coach McCulloch was yapping and Ozzie knew he had a job to do. Maybe tonight, when the blackness came again, he'd remember. That'd be real good. And then tomorrow he'd call Jess and write to Pop and things would be all right.

The third Shooter carried off was Malivai. He didn't have dozens of hands underneath his legs and back, just two trainers carrying the front and back of the stretcher. The doc had already prodded and poked and looked into his eyes and said, "It looks like the ACL," and Malivai knew that the gift that let him run faster than fire was gone. God had taken it back and He must have a reason, though it wasn't apparent to Malivai right then, not when the papers for his college scholarship were sitting on his desk at home, unsigned.

chapter 31

The next morning Ozzie was home in Yuranigh. He could hear birds singing and cows bellowing. Pop'd be up already, of course, and there'd be a cuppa and porridge waiting. But Ozzie woke up for real when he heard a phone ringing.

Alison brought it in. "It's from Australia."

"Hey," said Jess.

"G'day," said Ozzie. "To hear you it's so . . . good." As well as still being half-asleep, Ozzie had mild concussion.

"I've missed you."

Ozzie wanted to say something, but nothing came into his head.

"Listen." Jess hesitated. "Pop's in hospital. Mrs. Allan was going to ring but I wanted to do it. He's okay, just tired, we think. I just wanted you to know."

"What happened?"

"He passed out—fixing fences. Johnno found him.

236

The doctor reckons it was probably heatstroke, but they're keeping him in to make sure."

A pause. "I should come home, eh?"

"No. He's gonna be fine. If there's any news I'll call you straightaway."

"Promise?"

"I promise. Look, tell me how you're doing? Do you like America?"

"Yeah. It's real good."

"You figured out what you want to do next year?"

Ozzie paused. "Not yet. Though this college over here wants me to play for 'em. They're even talking about a scholarship. Pretty funny, eh?"

She didn't laugh. "That's probably who's been ringing, then."

"What?"

"Some Yankee fella has rung up Wazza, asking about you. You gonna go?"

"Nah. Course not."

A longer pause.

"I'd better get going," she finally said. "You look after yourself."

"Jess, I . . ." He didn't know what else to say.

"See ya, Ozzie."

*****

The first song of the homecoming dance was dedicated to one couple, the queen and her king. Unity and Sam were whistled at as they approached the floor to a slow love song. They held each other tight and swayed, while others looked on jealously, wishing it were them.

Halfway through the song the DJ called the rest of the Queen's Court onto the floor, so Ozzie and Angela, Jose and Braidie, and Tex and Leesa joined in. Angela's painted smile barely disguised her disappointment. "If I didn't come from Denham I think I would've won," she said to Ozzie. "Unity's lived here all her life so maybe the committee was . . . predisposed."

Ozzie didn't really understand what she meant, but he still had a headache so he didn't bother asking for an explanation. The music sped up and he started spinning and twisting Angela, trying to get her mind off losing. But it wasn't long before she disappeared, and Ozzie went over to Malivai, moved the crutches off the seat beside him, and sat down.

"How is it?" Ozzie asked, nodding at Mal's knee.

Malivai shook his head. He looked about as happy as Angela.

"You know," said Ozzie, "there's this famous footy player back home who broke his arm, not once or twice but four times. The last time he smacked straight into the goalposts. Bang! They had to put a steel rod in it and everything. Anyway, he went on to play for Australia, a real legend he was. And if he can do it . . . "

"Thanks, man," said Malivai.

They clasped hands. "Keep your chin up, mate."

Unity suddenly appeared and grabbed Ozzie. "Come on, twinkle toes. My turn!"

Ozzie had been dragged to enough old-time dances by his grandfather to know a thing or two about moving to music. A Buddy Holly song was playing and Ozzie led a laughing Unity through the four-step. A slow song was next and Ozzie tried to slip away, but Unity pulled him back to the floor. "You're not getting out of it that easy."

She held him close and Ozzie could feel people watching. The homecoming queen with the guy who'd thrown the winning pass; it was a good story. Ozzie could feel Unity's back through her soft dress and he wondered if there could be a happy ending. Angela was a stunner, but Unity, she was beautiful. A part of him wished they could go back to the water tower together, maybe even tonight.

Suddenly, someone tapped him on the back. Ozzie turned around and saw Sam, who wasn't smiling. Ozzie let go of Unity. If a fight had to happen, it had to happen. He couldn't really blame Sam, either. If Ozzie saw another bloke holding Jess so close, he'd probably want to beat the hell out of him.

Those around stopped dancing and watched as Sam grabbed Ozzie around the shoulders.

Ozzie tried to move but couldn't. *God, he's strong,* he thought.

Sam lifted Ozzie in the air and held him there.

Ozzie tensed his muscles, waiting to be thrown halfway across the room.

Instead Sam yelled, "Yee-hah! We goddamn did it!"

Pandemonium broke out on the dance floor—people hollering and screaming, all celebrating the win of the season, the win of a lifetime. Someone ran in, yelling "They found it! They found it!" and Coach McCulloch entered with the district trophy in his hands. Everybody rushed over to touch it, and in the excitement Sam dropped Ozzie onto the floor.

Before Ozzie's head was stomped on—which was the last thing he needed—Jose helped him up. "We did it, amigo. We really did it."

chapter 32

The *Hope Times* broke the bad news. Because it was a three-way tie between Hope, Denham, and the Booth Bears, and only the top two teams were allowed to represent the district in the state play-offs, one team would have to be eliminated. By a coin toss.

The toss was to be held at an undisclosed location, with a coin being thrown by each head coach. If there were two heads and one tail, the team with the tail would be eliminated. If two tails and one head landed, the head would be eliminated. If all three coins were heads or tails, the coins would be tossed again. This was one contest where you didn't want to be the odd head or tail out.

The location would be kept a secret to stop thousands of fans congregating and possibly fighting when things didn't go their way. There was one thing for sure, the newspaper said, "there's going to be one brokenhearted West Texas town."

Hope began preparing the best way it knew. Prayer groups were organized, and a special coin was chosen and blessed.

The day before the big event, Miss Simms showed up in history and asked for Ozzie to be excused. She took him to see Principal Fraser, who looked up from his giant desk and waved Ozzie in. Coach McCulloch was leaning against a bookshelf that had hardly any books but plenty of photos—photos of Mr. Fraser hunting, Mr. Fraser fishing, and Mr. Fraser with a football team, this year's team, in fact. The first team of district champions while he was principal.

"Austin, how are you, boy?" said Mr. Fraser.

"Good."

"Great game last Friday."

"Thanks."

"How's the head?"

"All right."

Mr. Fraser looked at Coach McCulloch, then back at Ozzie. "Austin, there's a few rumors doing the rounds, which isn't surprising at this time of year. People get awful strange around play-off time, hey, Coach?"

Ozzie hardly noticed the way Mr. Fraser said *tahh*me anymore.

Coach didn't say anything.

"Anyway," continued Mr. Fraser, "the Denham principal called me this morning, and although what he said is probably crazy I need to check it out. Okay?"

Ozzie nodded, though he didn't know what was going on.

Coach McCulloch suddenly stood up straight.

"Okay," said Mr. Fraser, "let me start by giving you some background information. All high-school and college sports in this country are amateur. Do you know what amateur means, Austin?"

"Not professional, right? Like Rugby Union used to be."

"Well, I'm not sure about rugby, but you're correct. It means that players can't get paid for their athletic endeavors. They may get certain expenses covered, like a travel allowance, but there are strict rules, and if they're broken, the player and the team he plays for get into a lot of trouble. Do you understand this?"

Ozzie nodded.

"Now, the Denham football coach has heard from some of their players that you were paid to play rugby in Australia . . ."

Ozzie went to speak but Mr. Fraser cut him off. "I strongly suggest you don't say anything until I'm finished, okay?"

Coach McCulloch had turned white.

Ozzie nodded. He was just going to say that he played Rugby League, not rugby.

"Anyway, I told the Denham principal that you played for your high-school team in . . ." Mr. Fraser looked at a sheet of paper. ". . . Yuranigh. And that you weren't paid any money whatsoever to play there. Is this correct?"

Ozzie nodded.

"You'll need to answer, son," said Mr. Fraser.

"Yeah, it is."

"And any other football that you might have played was simply an unorganized competition, like a fun pickup game, for instance."

Ozzie grimaced. "I did play for a club, as well."

"I wasn't aware of that." Mr. Fraser pulled at his tie. "Okay, let me say this. If, in those club games, any money was given to you to play, then not only would you be ineligible to play further high-school or college football, but the whole team would be penalized severely. Do you understand?"

"Yeah."

"Okay, so tell me, Austin, and I need you to be completely honest here, have you ever made any money from playing football?"

There was a pause.

Coach McCulloch started thinking about what it would be like to go back into the classroom, because no one would hire a football coach who'd been caught cheating.

Mr. Fraser pulled at his tie some more.

Ozzie finally answered. "Nah." It was true, too. The $150 he got per game all went to his grandfather, and his bonus for making the Grand Final went to a Mexican policeman.

Coach McCulloch breathed out and Mr. Fraser closed his eyes, then spoke again.

"Austin, it's very important that you tell no one about our discussion here today. Understand?"

Ozzie nodded.

* * * * *

Mr. Fraser had Miss Simms hand deliver a confidential memo to the Denham principal. "An investigation by school authorities finds there is no evidence to suggest that any Hope player has ever received money in a professional sporting capacity. Coin toss should go ahead as planned."

An hour later the Denham principal called. "Sorry, Frase," he said. "But we're gonna play hardball on this."

"Goddamn it, Chase!" said Mr. Fraser. "Can't you handle a licking once every fifteen years?"

"Only when that licking's a fair one," said Chase Biggs. "We've set up a meeting. Tonight at seven in the mayor's chambers."

"Hope or Denham?"

"Denham. Don't worry, there'll be no press. And we're not bringing in the county athletic director. Not yet."

"Goddamn it, Chase! Who *are* you bringin'?"

"Just me, Coach, and Jed Stanwich."

"The lawyer?"

"Just an interested observer, tonight."

"Goddamn!"

"You'll be going to hell if you keep that up, Frase."

Mr. Fraser slammed the phone down. "*You* go to hell!"

chapter 33

After short pleasantries, which weren't all that pleasant, the meeting got underway. Like most places of politics, this room had seen more than its share of mind games, scheming, and skulduggery, and tonight would be no exception. The men from Denham sat on the far side of the mahogany table, leaving the chairs closest to the entrance for the visitors. It was an old mafia trick: sit facing the door so you can't get shot in the back.

Strike one.

The three Hope men—Principal Gordon Fraser, Coach Ben McCulloch, and Attorney at Law Errol Simmons (for job-security reasons both the coach and the principal preferred not to get the mayor and the pastor involved)—were tieless. The Denham connection wore dark silk ties that matched their black jackets and polished black leather shoes.

Strike two.

A small tape recorder sat in the center of the table. "Gentlemen, the tape you are about to listen to is a backup, of course," said Jed Stanwich, a Denham liquidation lawyer who made his fortune when many Texas oil companies went belly-up in the late 1980s. "The original is in an envelope addressed to the county athletic director."

He pressed Play.

Strike three.

"Warren Ross, Empire Hotel," said an Australian, answering a phone.

"Hello, Mr. Ross, my name's Don Morgan. I work for a Texas newspaper." It was an American voice and Errol Simmons thought he recognized it. Probably one of Stanwich's cronies, he decided.

"Texas, Queensland?" said the Aussie.

"No. Texas in the United States of America."

"United who?"

"States of America. You know, the country."

"Oh, right. Sorry, mate. What's a Yank ringing me for?"

"I was wondering if you know a boy named Austin Eaton?"

The voice became friendlier. "Ozzie? Yeah, course. Jack's grandson."

"Good. Well, Austin's having a lot of success here on the football field. Did you know that?"

"Ozzie? Playing footy in America? I had no bloody idea."

"Well, I'm just calling for some background information on Austin. I heard that he plays rugby for a team that you own."

There was a laugh. "No, mate. I don't own 'em. I own the pub and we sponsor 'em. Buy their jerseys and stuff."

"What team is it?"

"The Yuranigh Magpies. Ozzie helped us make the Grand Final this year. Bloody brilliant, that kid."

There was a pause. "I heard it's a pretty good league he's playing in. Professional?"

"Most of the blokes play for fun, but there's a bit of money in it."

"So you pay Austin for playing?"

"Just pocket money, really. One fifty a game, but he's worth a lot more."

"So he makes one hundred and fifty dollars a game playing rugby?"

"That's what I just said. Look, who are you again, mate?"

"Don Morgan."

"And you're a journalist?"

"That's right."

"What paper do you work for?"

"Umm. The *Texas Post*."

Jed Stanwich hit the stop button.

Coach McCulloch spoke. "I've lived in Texas my whole life and I ain't heard of no *Texas Post*."

"I've seen some low things in my time but this is lower than a rattlesnake in the grass," growled Principal Fraser.

The Denham coach stood up. "Then tell me, what do you call recruiting a professional athlete to play for your school?"

"That's unfair and you know it!" said Coach McCulloch, standing and leaning across the table, finger pointing at the rival coach. "We had no idea the kid played rugby and made, what, a hundred and fifty dollars a game? Whoop-de-doo!"

"He's a pro, Ben. You know and I know it's illegal as all hell."

"You have five players who run the forty in under four and a half seconds. If anyone's recruiting professionals it's you boys with your crooked district line."

All three Denham men got to their feet.

"You take that back or I'll shove my hand so far down your throat you'll be shittin' knuckles!" said the Denham coach.

"You can't coach a lick so I'm pretty sure you can't fight, either," snapped Coach McCulloch.

The Denham coach suddenly jumped up on the mahogany table. The principal and Jed Stanwich grabbed an ankle each to try and stop him from killing the Shooter coach.

Coach McCulloch had his arms outstretched. He didn't

believe in fighting, but this was one time he'd gladly make an exception. He'd endured the ugly face coming toward him for fifteen defeats in a row, goddamn if he'd let these people take his one sweet victory away without a fight.

Errol Simmons, the Hope lawyer who hadn't said a word, shouted, "STOP IT! ALL OF YOU!"

The men looked at him.

Errol spoke quietly into the sudden silence. "Let's sit down and work this out like civilized people. If I want Jerry Springer, I'll turn on the TV."

Grudgingly, everyone returned to their seats.

"We've got a situation here and I'm sure it can be resolved," Errol said. "What are you men proposing?"

Jed Stanwich answered. "We want Hope to turn themselves in to the county athletic director."

"You've got to be kidding," said Principal Fraser. "He'd shut us down."

Errol put his hand out. "I'm sure there's another way. I don't think Denham would like it if, say, someone hired a team of private investigators to take a look at their program, see what they could turn up."

"You'd find nothing," said Chase Biggs, the Denham principal.

Errol looked up at the paintings of Denham mayors on the wall. These men knew a thing or two about playing political hardball. So did Errol. "So if, say, I asked the teachers why not one football star has failed a subject in twenty years, which would of course have made them ineligible to play, they'd tell me it's because they're all such fine students?"

"Yes, they would," said Biggs.

"And if I asked Mr. Garnett, who, if my memory serves me correctly, resigned last year as head of math, he'd say the same thing?"

Chase Biggs didn't reply. He took a sip of water instead.

"Errol's right," said Stanwich. "I'm certain we can come up with a better alternative."

"And don't tell me," said Principal Fraser. "You just happen to have one."

"As a matter of fact, I do," said Stanwich. He gave a little smirk. "Now we all know if this tape was given to the county AD all hell would break loose. The Shooters would have to forfeit all the games that Austin played in, which was every game this year, and they might even be kicked out of the competition."

Principal Fraser's lips tightened. Without a winning football program his school would be just like any other school, except worse.

Stanwich continued. "And if the press were to get ahold of this, the towns of Denham and Hope might declare war against each other."

The men nodded. On this one point they all agreed.

"So what I'm suggesting is that the tape never sees the light of day. If that happens, Hope keeps its tie for the district championship."

"What's the catch?" said Coach McCulloch.

Errol held up his hand, stopping the coach from saying any more.

"Well," said Jed Stanwich, "all we ask is that Hope lose the coin toss tomorrow night. Then Denham and Booth move through to the play-offs, everyone sympathizes with Hope for their rotten luck, and no one need be any the wiser."

"No deal," said Errol. "You lose the tape and we'll lose a certain math teacher's phone number. Everyone here knows he resigned from Denham when he was told that all first-string football players must pass their exams. I hear he's dying to tell his side of the story."

Stanwich grinned. "Errol, it's a nice try but I happened to talk to Garnett this afternoon. He's got a good job up there in Arkansas. He's happy to let bygones be bygones and he told me so. Lose the coin toss or lose the season. It's your choice."

There was silence for a few moments. No matter how bitter this proposal was to Hope, the alternative tasted a hundred times worse.

"How do you deliberately lose a coin toss?" asked Principal Fraser.

Stanwich stopped grinning. "We have a plan."

chapter 34

Unlucky Shooters Miss Play-offs

By Brent Sherlock
TIMES Sports Writer

If only we were bears.

A fairy-tale season came to an end last night when a coin landed the wrong way up in a freeway diner.

Finishing in a three-way tie, the Booth Bears, Denham Armadillos, and Hope Shooters couldn't all advance to the state play-offs. One team had to be eliminated by a coin toss, and so when the respective high-school football coaches showed up they did so with white knuckles and the knowledge that a dream would end for a town.

In an unusual break from convention the coaches didn't throw at the same time. Coach Chuck Creely from Booth went first and came up heads, as did Coach Mal Shield from Denham. Coach Ben McCulloch, who was last, reached into his left pocket, took out a nickel, and took in a deep breath. For a moment he held the coin up to his eyes, as if in prayer, knowing that he needed heads to force a retoss.

It came up tails.

"We had a heck of a season," said Coach McCulloch. "Going 8 and 1 and tying for a district championship is something I'm awfully proud of. I hope everyone in Hope feels the same."

The Shooters' players were gathered at team captain Tex Powell's house, glued to the radio. Many openly wept when the result came through.

"It totally sucks, man," said Powell. "We could've gone all the way this year."

The Hope community has offered their condolences and support. Julie Slipper from the school board said that Coach McCulloch has been offered an increased salary and the opportunity to hire a new offensive coordinator. The coach was not available for comment. Slipper also said that a pep rally would be held on Tuesday night to congratulate the players, whose 8–1 regular season record is the best in sixteen years.

For Hope fans, however, this will be little consolation. For the first time in a long time a Shooters team seemed capable of playing for a state title. The trouble is, when the postseason starts, they won't be there.

According to well-known booster Dave Graham, there is only one option. "After the pep rally we go into hibernation and don't wake up till next season."

If only we were bears.

In related news:
—Malivai Thomas underwent a major knee reconstruction to repair his anterior cruciate ligament last night. The surgeon said that, although the operation was a success, it will be a long, hard road back for Thomas and there is no guarantee he will ever regain his blinding speed. At present Thomas is unsure of his future in football. Since the injury, no

college has expressed an interest in signing him.
—Sam Wilson and Austin Eaton are taking a
recruiting trip to Justice University this weekend.
The Eagles are interested in both Shooter stars.

chapter 35

The gymnasium at Justice University is almost as big as a football field. In fact, in the middle of the gym *is* a quarter of a football field, where the green grass is artificial along with the cool breeze—a welcome escape from the summer sun.

The rest of the gym is filled with free weights, power racks, chin-up bars, exercise bikes that beep, giant rubber balls, and lots, lots more. Signs on the wall display lifting records that are all held by footballers, because at Justice, footballers are the biggest and the strongest. They're also the only athletes eligible to hold lifting records.

Before he'd come to America the only place Ozzie had lifted weights was in the old dairy, where he had a wooden bench, a bar, and four forty-pound round weights. He'd become used to things being bigger and better over here, but this . . . Imagine how much muscle Johnno could put on here in a month?

"Pretty cool, ain't it?" said Andy Hosking, the student who'd been assigned to show Ozzie around. "Not much like this back home."

Ozzie looked at Andy. "Where are you from?"

"Australia. *Cah*n't you tell?"

Ozzie did his best not to laugh. Andy sounded about as Australian as Greg Norman. "What part?"

"Sydney. You?"

"Yuranigh."

"The outback?"

"Sort of." Ozzie couldn't get over the way this bloke talked. "How long you been here?"

"I'm a junior, so just over two years. They offered me a golf scholarship and I jumped at it. It's an awesome school. You'll love it."

To Ozzie, a junior was a youngster, school was a place you went to before university, and awesome was a word you didn't use when describing school. He wondered whether he'd talk like this if he lived here a few more years. Would he become someone another Aussie didn't recognize?

"We've got some cool stuff lined up for you," said Andy. "A sorority party tonight and some boosters are taking you to the Steakhouse for lunch tomorrow. Those cows melt in your mouth, dude."

Andy showed Ozzie around the rest of the university, including the athletes-only dining room, the athletes-only dorm rooms, and the athletes-only games room. Athletes could go for their whole four years at university and meet regular students only in class.

The athletics department was housed inside the college's seventy-thousand-seat football stadium. There were hundreds of offices and huge tutorial rooms designed to make sure athletes passed their classes and stayed eligible to play sports for Justice. Ozzie was introduced to dozens of smiling faces that said, "So pleased to *meet* you! Hope to see you next year!"

One of the offices was bigger than all the others and it wasn't the athletic director's. The door to it opened and out walked the head football coach with his arm around Sam Wilson's shoulder. Both were smiling.

"Coach Lee, this is Austin Eaton," said Andy.

"I surely know that," said Coach Lee, shaking Ozzie's hand. The coach wore an Eagle T-shirt, which showed a stomach fat from too much barbeque but stretched tight from years of sit-ups.

He turned to Sam. "Son, I'd like to see you real soon."

"Thanks, Coach," said Sam. He leaned in close to Ozzie. "Good luck, mate."

Coach Lee ushered Ozzie into his office. Mounted on the wall above his chair was a deer's head, and on the other walls were photographs of football players, and banners saying Conference Champions.

"Have a seat," said Coach Lee. "How's it all going so far?"

"Good."

"What's impressed you the most? The purdy college girls?"

Ozzie smiled. "The weight room."

"It's somethin', innit? I've seen boys go in there, 150, 160 pounds . . ." The head coach sat back and studied Ozzie. "About the same as you. They spend a summer in the weight room and"—he clicked his fingers—"they're 200 pounds. Not boys anymore but men. You won't find too many people wanna mess with that much muscle. Your daddy a big man?"

"Not huge, but real strong. Still can't beat him in an arm wrestle." Ozzie didn't realize that he wasn't talking about his father but his grandfather.

"You spend some time in our weight room and I guarantee you'll pin his arm to the table so quick he won't ask for a rematch." Coach Lee laughed briefly, then became serious. "Look, Austin, let me get right to it. Our recruiters have been watching you all season. Most boys we study for two or three years, so you were a surprise package, I'll admit. But with you, right away we liked what we saw. You're not the quickest or the biggest, but you've got something the others don't. You *know* football. I don't see that often, especially not from an Australian." He shook his head. "Look, I just want to know one thing. What do you love about the game? The most? Because I believe it's the things we love that tell us who we are."

Ozzie looked up and saw a black-and-white photo of a player diving to make a catch. The player's eyes were on the ball, his body stretched horizontally, three feet off the ground. "When I'm out there, I don't have to think about anything. I can just . . . play."

"I know exactly what you mean. Best form of meditation I ever had was being handed the ball on fourth and one with three linebackers heading straight for me." The coach gave a wistful smile. "But that was a long time ago. Now I get paid a million dollars a year to run a football team and you know what I tell my players? It's worry money. I get paid to worry about all the things that can go wrong so the players don't have to. All they need to do is pass their classes and play football. What more could a young man want? But you know what? Not many of them can do it. They worry about being a starter, about winning, about making it to the pros, about which cheerleader they're gonna date. But it's boys like you who I want. Boys who can let me do the worrying for them. Boys who can stay in the moment and just play. Sometimes I think America has got too much on its mind to be great these days."

Coach Lee locked eyes with Ozzie. "Now I know you are a big-time rugby player as well, but I'd love to have you here as part of our program. In front of me is a piece of paper with your name on it, with an offer of a full scholarship for four years to Justice University. That's housing, meals, books, tuition, and the chance to play football for one of the finest college teams in the country. Now, I know you haven't been here too long, but let me tell you, any boy from Texas or nearly the whole of the USA would jump at this opportunity. After four years, if you're good enough, there's always the chance of a professional contract. We had a boy last year who signed with the Dallas Cowboys for $20 million. But even if that doesn't happen, you'll leave here with an education you can use anywhere in the world and memories that will last a lifetime. I don't need an answer straightaway but I will need one soon. You think about it."

When they walked out of the office, the coach put his arm around Ozzie, fingers squeezing a shoulder. "Son, I hope to see you real soon."

There was another boy waiting to come in.

* * * * *

The gathering at the Alpha Gamma Pi sorority house wasn't called a party but a "mixer." Whether this referred to people or drinks Ozzie wasn't sure, because the under-twenty-one no-drinking law didn't seem to apply. Every room was stocked with hard, soft, and middle-of-the-road liquor, the only restriction being that partygoers had to drink out of large red plastic cups. Girls wore makeup like war paint and guys raised two fists and screamed "YEE-AHHH!" when someone opened his throat and chugged.

"Athletes get a free pass to any frat or sorority party," Andy said to Ozzie. "Just think, man. Next year this could be you every weekend."

Andy disappeared for a minute. He brought back Julie. "Another Aussie," he said. "A tennis player." Andy swung an imaginary racket and nearly knocked the drink out of her hand. "She can really smack that ball."

"G'day," said Ozzie.

They shook hands. "It's good to hear your voice," said Julie. "I'm so homesick it's not funny."

A guy beside them chugged a full plastic cup and Andy raised two fists and yelled "YEAH!"

"You wanna talk outside?" Ozzie asked Julie.

She nodded.

They found a couple of seats near the pool. It was early November and the nights had become cool, but sorority money buys outside heaters that shine like giant cigarettes.

"How long you been here?" asked Ozzie.

"Two months. Just getting used to it. The first week I cried like a baby. Still do, some nights."

"It's different, eh?"

"Yeah, but not that different. I don't know what I was expecting, but you walk down the street here and you see McDonald's, KFC, Subway—it's almost the same as walking down the main street of Wagga, where I'm from."

"Except here you don't see kangaroos jumping down the main street."

She folded her arms across her chest. "You don't have 'em in Wagga, either. Well, not every day."

They laughed.

"Why do you miss home, then?" said Ozzie.

"I miss my mum and dad." She sighed. "I miss other stuff, too. It *is* different here, I don't know how, but it is."

Ozzie looked at the pool and saw himself, the water a mirror.

"Why'd you come to America?" Julie asked.

"On an exchange."

"Yeah, but why?"

He thought for a moment. No one had ever asked him that before. "I'm from a small place, and when my grandfather was my age he went overseas, to war. He always talked about it like it was this great adventure." Ozzie looked back into the water. "I finished school and was gonna move to Brisbane, but . . ." He shrugged.

"Tell me."

"My best mate and girlfriend were still around and I wanted to help my pop on the farm. This lady, Mrs. Allan, said I could stay in Yuranigh for the mustering season and come to America after that. It sounded like a good deal."

There was a slight gap between Julie's top two front teeth. Ozzie would never have noticed it back in Australia, but here he was becoming used to perfection.

"Why'd you come?" he asked.

"I wanted to see what America was like, I s'pose," said Julie. "Every afternoon after school I used to watch *Happy Days*. I loved that show. They always looked so . . . happy." She grinned and so did Ozzie. "I could've gone straight onto the pro tennis circuit. I won the Australian Junior title and everything. But I wanted to check this place out. All because of bloody *Happy Days*."

"Aaaayyy," said Ozzie, putting his thumb in the air.

Julie slapped him on the shoulder.

There were other small groups settled around the pool. Ozzie saw what looked to be one body lying on a long plastic deck chair slowly disentwine into two and stand up. The couple walked past, hand in hand, probably on their way to an upstairs bedroom.

The girl was stunning, her tangled hair only making her more beautiful.

The boy was Sam.

chapter 36

American steaks are different from Australian steaks. They're thicker, tenderer, and a lot more fatty. While tucking into his prime rib, Ozzie asked the boosters why the steaks were like they were. He knew his grandfather would be interested.

"We pump steroids into 'em," said the one sitting next to him, who owned a ranch.

"Really?" said Ozzie.

"You bet. Same as our linemen."

There was a second of silence.

"That was a joke," said the man.

On the other side of Ozzie was a younger booster, who did most of the talking, his favorite buzzwords being *contacts* and *opportunity*. Many of the boosters were businessmen who loved football and football players, he said. In fact, he was a football player himself, "walking on" to the team in the early nineties. He didn't play a whole lot of football but he did do a whole lot of networking, and now he was making $250,000 a year "walking on" to businesses in financial trouble and taking them over. "You use your contacts while you are here, boys, and an opportunity will present itself. Just look at me."

After lunch he showed Ozzie and Sam his new supercharged SVT Ford Mustang Cobra. Under the hood was a 390-horsepower, V-8 engine, and in the trunk were presents. "By law we can't give you much, but here's some things we can give you," he said, taking high-top basketball shoes, T-shirts, and hats out of the trunk. "Sometimes other gifts have a way of showing up, too. If they do, don't ask why, just take 'em. Whether you boys decide to come here or not."

On the bus ride home Ozzie tried on the shoes. The right one was a perfect fit, but his big toe rammed against something hard in the left. It was a black box. Sam found one, too. Inside the boxes were watches, with Rolex written on them, and because the second-hand moved smoothly and quietly around the face rather than tick, second by second, Sam knew they were real. "Holy crap," he said. "You know what these are worth?"

"A few hundred?" said Ozzie.

"Try five thousand."

"But doesn't that make us professional?"

"Only if someone tells. And I don't think those guys will, do you?"

Ozzie looked out the window. A little girl sitting on a tricycle waved at him. "A lot of bullshit goes on in America, doesn't it?"

A woman in front turned round and gave Ozzie a stare.

"Sorry, ma'am," said Sam. "My friend needs to watch his mouth."

"He surely does," said the woman. "Some of us passengers are Christian people."

She turned around and Sam raised a middle finger to her back. "What do you mean?" he asked Ozzie.

"People here say one thing and do another. Like, you'll probably go home and tell Unity you love her."

"I do love her."

"You have a funny way of showing it."

"It's just . . ." Sam lowered his voice. "Goddamn America, man. There's so many women."

"The land of opportunity?"

The irony was lost on Sam. "Exactly. I'll marry Unity one day, you'll see. But right now I'm young and . . . You have a girlfriend back home?"

"Yeah."

"You love her?"

Ozzie looked out the window again. A little boy pointed a toy gun at him and pretended to shoot. "Yeah."

"Does she know about Angela?"

Ozzie felt his new watch. Gold was heavier and softer than he thought it would be. "No."

"Then you know what I'm talking about."

Ozzie slipped on the Rolex. It felt cool on his skin. Suddenly he realized he'd lost his old watch, the one Jess had bought him before he left. Did he leave it in Mexico? At the Denham pool? He had no idea. He'd lost it without even realizing it was gone.

* * * * *

The next pep rally should have been held on the third Monday night of the following August, when a new football team would be welcomed in "The Beginning." Now, there was no game to look forward to, no town that coaches and players and fans could focus their hate on, no state championship that could be won. But because the season had ended so suddenly it felt wrong if the town didn't celebrate and commiserate together.

It felt wrong losing a coin toss. Although no one said it, everyone thought the same thing: perhaps it was God's will? And if so, why? But tonight wasn't a time for answers. The band played "Boogie Woogie Bugle Boy," the cheerleaders' skirts flew around their waists, and the team assembled for the last time. Some Hopettes, seated behind their players, had already caught the red-eyed bug, because not to cry on a night like tonight would be like not loving God or America, like not loving football.

Coach McCulloch stood up to speak and the crowd

rose and clapped like fans at a rock concert demanding an encore. No one in Hope—besides his wife—knew, and he certainly didn't intend to announce it here, but there wouldn't be one. He'd impressed enough of the right people to be offered a college coaching job. In the interview they'd asked him almost exclusively about the new offense he invented, and of course he humbly took the credit and confidently promised results. The Line Formation was his ticket up in the world of football. It was the break he'd been looking for and now he was hoping to recruit one person to help him succeed. The problem was that he couldn't recruit until he officially resigned as head coach of the Shooters, tomorrow. He just hoped that Ozzie didn't sign with Justice University before then.

The crowd sat.

"Ladies and gentlemen, when I stood here in August I looked into y'all's eyes and could see that some of you didn't believe." Because he was resigning the coach had nothing to lose. "There were doubts about whether or not I could coach, whether or not the team could win even a few games." He paused to make people feel uncomfortable, then, "I must admit, even I wasn't entirely sure." Laughter broke the tension. "Well, the young men sitting to my right proved me and all y'all wrong. It's my privilege to be standing up here today to celebrate an eight and one season. A season that should still be going if it weren't for a rigged coin toss." There was more laughter, people not realizing that the coach couldn't have been more serious. "Ladies and gentlemen, I give you the Hope Shooters."

The coach pointed to the team and the crowd stood again. The cheering lasted for minutes, and the Hopettes cried some more.

The three captains, Sam, Tex, and Malivai, went to the podium. Sam spoke first.

"This season has meant more to me than y'all can imagine. I always thought that as quarterback I had to win every game on my own. I tried to carry the world on my shoulders and it got real heavy. But a couple of things happened, a couple of *people* happened, and I learned to trust others, let 'em help me. No man is an island. I'm sure many of you knew that, but I didn't."

Tex was next. "One thing I'll never forget is the look on those Armadillo faces when we scored the last touchdown and beat their asses. Man, that's something I'm gonna cherish for the rest of my life."

Malivai was last. He leaned his crutches against the podium and didn't say a word, just stood in front of the microphone and did what he did best. He sang. What was once a traditional gospel song had become a call to end racial disharmony, and now it seemed to sum up a town and a people who wanted more than they'd got.

> *We shall overcome, we shall overcome*
> *We shall overcome some day*

Oh, deep in my heart, I do believe
We shall overcome some day

The Lord will see us through, the Lord will
*   see us through*
The Lord will see us through some day
Oh, deep in my heart, I do believe
The Lord will see us through some day

We're on to victory, we're on to victory
We're on to victory some day
Oh, deep in my heart, I do believe
We're on to victory some day

We'll walk hand in hand, we'll walk hand in hand
We'll walk hand in hand some day
Oh, deep in my heart, I do believe
We'll walk hand in hand some day

We are not afraid, we are not afraid
We are not afraid today
Oh, deep in my heart, I do believe
We are not afraid today

The truth shall make us free, the truth
*   shall make us free*
The truth shall make us free some day

Oh, deep in my heart, I do believe
The truth shall make us free some day

We shall live in peace, we shall live in peace
We shall live in peace some day
Oh, deep in my heart, I do believe
We shall live in peace some day.

When the captains sat down, the band played the school fight song and the pep rally should have been over. But the crowd wanted to hear one more person, so they started a chant: "Austin! Austin! Austin!"

He walked to the podium and there was silence. After Malivai's song hardly an eye was dry, but from Ozzie's no tears had fallen. When his dad left, his grandfather had told him to be a man and that men don't cry, so he never had.

But looking out at the people—at Unity, Sam, Angela, Malivai, Jose, Tex, everyone—something inside Ozzie snapped. There was so much emotion in this place. He could handle the gruff rebukes of Pop, the playful punches of Johnno, and the gentle but firm hand of Jess. He could recognize that as love. Maybe not the love of Hollywood movies he and Jess watched at the Yuranigh cinema on Saturday nights, but love all the same. But this? People who didn't even know him chanting his name because he could play footy? Crying because a football season was over?

Ozzie didn't say a word and he certainly didn't sing. The dam inside burst and the water exploded out and he had no idea why.

* * * * *

That night, Pop was driving a tractor and Ozzie was running alongside, trying to keep up. It must have been turbocharged because no matter how fast he ran, the tractor kept pulling ahead. Pop yelled at him to hurry the hell up, but the tractor got too far in front and Ozzie chased and chased until he couldn't see or hear Pop anymore.

When the phone woke him, he knew who it was and why they were calling. It could have been simple deduction—only someone living in another hemisphere would ring at three a.m. And when people ring at three a.m. it's usually bad news, unless they are drunk. But part of him already knew. He'd felt it at the pep rally and seen it in a dream.

Pop was dead.

POST-
GAME

★

chapter 37

Unity came to say good-bye, although she didn't know it was good-bye until she saw the bags. "Where're you going?"

"Home," said Ozzie.

"You're coming back, aren't you?"

"Dunno. My grandfather, he's . . ." Ozzie couldn't say it. They hugged.

"Listen," said Unity. "Next year, I'm going to Justice University." She looked him in the eye. "Come."

"Is Sam going?"

She looked away. "I don't know, and right now, I don't really care. We were out the other night and someone sent him a text. I think it was another girl."

Ozzie was quiet.

Her hands reached around his waist. "I know this isn't Australia but it's a great country, Austin. Not perfect, but still great. I think you'd be happy here."

Her lips brushed against his, the first stroke of a masterpiece. He felt like he'd died and gone to heaven.

* * * * *

"We all knew Jack Freeman," said Wazza, standing in front of a coffin.

The crematorium was one of the few air-conditioned buildings in Yuranigh. It seemed to be okay to let the kids sweat at school but not for the stiffs to sweat before their bodies were reduced to a pile of ashes. But right now the forty or so live bodies squeezed into the room, dressed in black, were extremely grateful.

"The only reason I'm up here is that, being the owner and bartender of the local pub, I probably heard him rant and rave more than most."

A few laughs.

"He was a good bloke. Went away to war in 1941, though if you listened to Jack he spent as much time wandering around Europe AWOL after a win at the two-up as he did fighting krauts.

"Married Jean when he returned, had a daughter, Kathy, and spent his life playing and watching footy, running beef cattle, and growing a few crops—when it rained. Liked a drink, can't deny that, but wasn't a violent drunk. Except when someone tried to say Aussie Rules was a better game than League."

Laughter again.

"But to those who knew him well, his life really turned around in the last ten years. He was always a good bloke but he became something special when young Ozzie moved in. Didn't drink much after that, stopped smokin', and started acting more mature. You'd think at that age he already would've been mature, but he always called himself a late bloomer, did Jack."

More a chuckle this time. With a few sniffles from the women.

"He loved nothing more than to watch Ozzie run out on the field and play footy, and I've never seen a prouder man than when Ozzie scored the winning try against Golda, even if the bloody ref was blind."

"Hear, hear," said a few voices.

"He said to anyone who'd listen that Ozzie'd play for Queensland Country one day. And he said it's because he taught the little bugger everything he knows."

A final outburst of laughter.

"He lived here a long time, had his share of fights and made his share of enemies, but whenever he walked down the main street he'd say g'day to everyone, and everyone'd say g'day to him. If there's a League team in heaven, Jack'll be packing down between the two front-rowers right now. Have a good one, Jack. We'll miss you."

"Hear, hear!"

The celebrant took over. "Ashes to ashes. Dust to dust.

What has sprung forth is now returned. What has lived here on earth will now live in eternal peace."

He nodded and someone pressed Play.

> *Oh there once was a swagman camped*
> *by a billabong,*
> *Under the shade of a Coolabah tree;*
> *And he sang as he looked at his old billy boiling,*
> *"Who'll come a-waltzing Matilda with me?"*
>
> *"Who'll come a-waltzing Matilda, my darling?*
> *Who'll come a-waltzing Matilda with me?*
> *Waltzing Matilda and leading a water-bag—*
> *Who'll come a-waltzing Matilda with me?"*

A few blokes from the RSL held caps over their uniformed hearts. They didn't all get along with Jack, but he had fought for his country in World War II and not many of those were left. "It was the world wars that made Australia," they'd say over a beer, later. "Taught a generation of men mateship and showed the world who this country was."

"Bloody rubbish," Jack would have replied, because he'd done it hundreds of times before. "War taught me nothing more than how to drink, gamble, and swear. Not to mention kill. It's you blokes who give war a good name. If there's another, I'll hide Ozzie out bush."

A few older women held tissues to their noses. They remembered when Jack's wife had left and never came back. It was the best piece of gossip they'd had in years. Later, when their own husbands started dropping like flies with heart attacks from too much cream, or drowning in flash floods trying to save livestock, or rolling their pickups driving home drunk, many had got to know Jack even better, at the old-time dances. Jack may not have been a smooth talker but he sure was a smooth dancer, and it wasn't easy seeing another good man waltz off into the sky.

Johnno looked on from the back row. He'd changed. The six-pack-of-beer pot-belly had been replaced by a six-pack of muscle, the skinny shoulders now wide and strong. He'd kept up his end of the bargain.

Jess was next to him, her long hair falling down her back. Ozzie snuck a glance and thought she was more beautiful than ever. Not her face or her body, but everything about her. Everything Ozzie had missed.

The day Ozzie had arrived home he had taken her to Jack's place. His place, now. They'd kissed but she didn't search deep into his mouth, the way she always had.

"Can you stay tonight?" asked Ozzie.

She shook her head. Just a little but enough.

"Why not?"

"Mum'll expect me home."

"She'll understand. Tell her we'll sleep in different rooms."

"She won't believe me."

"There's something else, isn't there?"

She didn't reply.

"Not . . . someone else?"

Tears rolled down her cheeks like fat raindrops. "I don't want to talk about it till after the funeral."

"I do."

She turned away.

"Who is it?"

Nothing.

He grabbed a soft shoulder and spun her. "WHO?"

She didn't look at him. "We didn't mean for it to happen. But you don't *need* anyone. You're so strong and . . ."

When Ozzie heard that, it was like a blow to the gut.

"And I thought you were gonna stay in America and . . ."

"Who?" His voice was soft, almost a whisper, pleading, though he wasn't really sure he wanted to know.

"He got his act together and he *needs* me. Wazza knows this bloke in Townsville who can get him a tryout with the Cowboys. I can go to James Cook uni and study early childhood and . . ."

"No," said Ozzie.

Jess was sobbing.

"Why? Of all the blokes, why'd you have to pick . . ." Ozzie stopped talking and focused on his breathing, like he did in footy when he corked a thigh or whacked his head. In and out. In and out. He wasn't going to cry over a girl.

"We didn't mean for it to happen," she said.

"Just go."

"Will you be all right?"

"Go."

As the casket dropped with a faint click, hate rose up inside Ozzie like bile. When the music stopped, Johnno approached. He didn't look into Ozzie's eyes and he didn't touch his ex-best friend. But he did say, "I'm sorry, mate. Real sorry. About everything."

Ozzie's hands turned into fists. He wanted to deck him, but he couldn't do it here. Not until he'd counted to ten.

"I love her," Johnno said.

"So did I." Ozzie looked at Jess but she didn't say anything, so he walked into the hot sun, jumped in Jack's truck, and left.

chapter 38

Walking across the soft turf Ozzie passed the cheerleaders practicing for the upcoming season. *Not bad*, he thought, as he watched them shake to music piped through stadium speakers. A girl saw him looking and smiled, so Ozzie smiled back. Yeah, they were good, but not as good as Unity and the girls, who really knew how to get people cheering.

A secretary showed Ozzie in and told him to wait. It had been a tough decision coming here. After the funeral Coach McCulloch had rung Mrs. Allan and left a message for Ozzie to call back, collect. When Ozzie did, Coach tried hard to convince him to go to Peters University. "I'm the new head coach," he said, "and I want the very first scholarship player I sign to be you. Just imagine the excitement of Hope and then double it. That's what it'll be like. You and me, son, let's ride this dream as far as it takes us."

Before Ozzie could reply, the coach put someone else on the phone. "Austin? It's me, Angela."

As if he didn't know.

"Listen, it's all been arranged. I'm going to Peters!" she said. "You've got to come, Austin, you just . . . gotta! We'll have *so* much fun together!"

He didn't know what to say, so he said the first thing that came into his head. "Why'd you tell 'em?"

"Excuse me?"

"Why'd you tell 'em about the money? From footy?"

"Austin, what are you talking about? I didn't tell anyone anything."

The line suddenly cut out, thanks to Ozzie's finger pressing the button.

Then there was Justice University. Ozzie had found the scholarship papers in his pocket and read through the promotional material. Last year's team had played a game on national television that had been watched by 20 million people. There was also a picture of the weight room, though Johnno proved you didn't need millions of bucks worth of equipment to put on muscle, just someone who believed in you. Still, it was a great opportunity, and Unity would be there.

His other option was to stay in Yuranigh, play for the local team, and be a farmer. Pop hadn't got around to selling up, and living the simple life didn't seem like such a bad idea to Ozzie, although the simple life wasn't nearly as simple as it was cracked up to be. Ozzie had seen enough droughts, floods, and heartache to know that. Wazza had helped him find a good head stockman—a bloke who just happened to be a handy league player as well. Soon, Ozzie might be joining him on the farm and in the team. But then again . . .

A man came out, shook hands, and took him into an office. "Hope you don't mind, but I like to ask a few questions, try and find out what makes you boys tick."

Ozzie didn't know whether to nod or shake his head. Those "hope you don't minds" were confusing.

"I don't know too much about you, but enough to realize that you've had a tough time of it lately. Life isn't always fair. I'm sorry about that."

Ozzie gave a quick nod.

"So, talking about life, who's been the biggest influence on yours?"

No small talk from this bloke, thought Ozzie. "Pop."

"What'd he teach you?"

"Umm." Ozzie looked up at the wall. There was a photo of a mountain, rising into blue sky. "Never fake a penalty. Be loyal to your mates. Don't punch someone till you count to ten."

The coach smiled. "Sounds like a wise fellow. And tell me about America. What's one thing you like about it?"

"They don't make you feel bad if you're good at somethin'."

"And something you don't like?"

Ozzie looked at the other wall. A photo of the ocean. Tight drops of rain were falling but the sun was out, illuminating the mist and blue of the sea. "Nothing's what it seems."

"What about Australia, then?"

"It's a lot like America. Lot more than I thought. I had a mate I wanted to come to Brisbane with me but he's gone to the Cowboys and taken my girlfriend."

"That's too bad." The coach leaned forward. "But remember something. What you take from America and what you leave behind is up to you. Your generation is the future of this country. You make it what you want it to be."

Ozzie listened.

"We've been real impressed with you, particularly in the trial games. Unlike a lot of young fellas, you're a team player. That's what we like the most."

"Thanks."

"And I'm going to give you a chance to join us, but only if you think you can do two things, okay?"

Ozzie's heart started racing but he tried to keep his voice steady. "Okay."

The coach looked into Ozzie's eyes. "One is that you be a contributor. In my life I see two types of people: contributors and blamers, and the best people are those that put in, day in, day out, to their team, their own lives, and their community. Yeah?"

"Yeah."

"And the only way you can contribute is if you're honest, so that's the second thing. I'd like you to be honest with everyone, but that's up to you, I guess. But I demand that you're honest with me. I don't care how good you are at footy, you tell me a lie and you're out. You tell me the truth, no matter how bad it is, and you've got nothing to worry about. Understand?"

Ozzie smiled because for once, he did.

The coach shook Ozzie's hand. "Welcome to the Brisbane Broncos."

* * * * *

Dear Austin,

Howdy! I was so sad to hear you're not coming back but feel lucky for the chance to have met you. I'd really like for us to write and stay friends, and maybe one day you might visit, or I might even go "down under" and see you. You never know, I might just show up at your door, soon!

Let me start by giving you all the Hope gossip. For some reason there was this big crackdown on cheating after you left. Jose did an American Ethics subject and some kid stole the test and passed it around.

Someone found out and all the students who used the stolen test got put on academic probation, which means that Jose can't go to college next year! He's going to work, save up money, and then apply, so hopefully he'll get there in the end. But it's so stupid, seeing he's one of the smartest people in our school and all.

Talking about college, Malivai has decided not to go. Can you believe that? Since he hurt his knee he's been acting real strange, and then he told me that he finally figured out why God made him lose his scholarship. It's so he can sing. He's trying out for the next American Idol and he thinks God will make him win! You know how good he is at singing so he's got a chance, but I told him to go to college <u>and</u> go on Idol, but he won't listen.

Angela has also been acting kinda weird. After you left she started dating her ex-boyfriend from Denham and they're both going to Peters next year. She's been bragging about how she got a cheerleading scholarship, even though tryouts aren't held until April. God knows how she managed that. I'm sorry if any of this upsets you, but I thought you'd want to know. I knew she still held a torch for the Denham boy—he's a real good football player, got a scholarship and everything.

291

Sam's going to Justice so it looks like we'll be together awhile longer. He says hi and hopes you change your mind so you two can play together again. He says he'd like to teach you how to really throw a football, but I tell him you already can!

Hope is still the same. No one's forgotten you, and if you come back I bet they'd throw some sort of parade. Us seniors are looking forward to leaving for college, but the juniors are excited about next year's football team. Do you know that Coach Hayes has agreed to help out the team again? He's going to mentor the new coach. Everyone's real thrilled about it.

Hope you're enjoying Australia and getting everything you want out of life. We sure are missing you here.

Love and kisses (don't tell Sam!)

Unity
xxx

PS The Grahams send their love.

chapter 39

In a hotel room in Sydney the phone rang. Ozzie picked it up warily. He'd already been pranked by one of the senior members of the team, who'd pretended to be from *The Footy Show*.

"Ozzie, that you?"

"G'day, Mr. Conroy." Ozzie felt pretty confident this call was legit. You'd have to be a professional impersonator to imitate the old man's gravelly voice.

"Listen, I just wanted to wish you best of luck for tomorrow," said Cyril.

"Thanks."

"How're you feeling?"

"A few butterflies."

Cyril chuckled. "I still remember my first game. Not much money and no TV back then, but I was so nervous I couldn't sleep a wink. In the middle of the night my roommate gave me a few glasses of whiskey to calm me down, and then they couldn't bloody wake me up in the morning! Played the first half with a splitting headache."

Ozzie laughed. He missed hearing stories like that.

"Listen, Ozzie, I'm in Yuranigh for the junior carnival. There's a few people here who want to say hello."

Mrs. Allan was first. "Now, Austin, make sure your socks are pulled up tomorrow, and comb your hair, too. There'll be a lot of people watching. You can at least look the part."

Ozzie smiled. "Yes, Mrs. Allan."

"And all the ladies at Rotary said to say hello, and we've posted some Anzac cookies to your apartment in Brisbane. They should be there when you get back."

"Thanks, Mrs. Allan."

Next was Wazza. "How are you, champ?"

"Good."

"Ready to knock 'em dead?"

"I'll give it a go."

"I'm sure you will. I just want to say that your pop would've been proud of you. No, I take that back. He *is* proud of you. I'm sure he'll be looking down tomorrow yelling, 'For God's sake, son, pass it!'"

Ozzie laughed.

"We're all looking forward to the game. Now, no pressure or anything, but the boys from the club have roped me into a deal. If you score a try, I have to put on free beers for the rest of the game. So if you do score, make it the second half, okay?"

Ozzie laughed. "I'll do my best."

And finally it was back to Cyril. "Listen, when you get out there everything will seem like it's in fast motion. First grade footy, it's a bit like life in the big city. Try and get involved early, get a touch, make a tackle, anything. After that you'll be fine."

"Thanks, Mr. Conroy. It means a lot."

"You're a special talent, Ozzie. I knew it the first day I saw you. Didn't always want to believe it, but deep down I knew how good you were."

After the call Ozzie watched television, hoping to take his mind off the game, hoping to settle his stomach. An American drama was on, one of those shows where someone dies at the start of every episode and someone is caught and thrown in prison for life at the end. Ozzie didn't watch much television but liked to escape every now and then, especially when he was playing with and against some of his Rugby League heroes in less than a day.

There was a scream and the camera zoomed in for a close-up of a dead body—a young woman, blood trickling out of her ear.

Suddenly Ozzie sat up straight. "I know that girl!" he said to his hotel roommate, another country boy—from Cherbourg—making it big in the city.

"Who? The dead one?" said the roommate.

"Yeah."

"Where from?"

Ozzie searched his mind but couldn't place her. "I'm not sure. But I know I know her."

"Yeah, and I know Britney Spears," said the roommate.

An ad came on. "What time are we flying out after the game?" asked the roommate.

And suddenly Ozzie smiled, because he knew exactly who the dead girl was.

She was the girl from the plane.

chapter 40

It was a short walk from the dressing room, but long enough for a lot of things to race through Ozzie's mind. He saw flashes of Friday nights in Texas, walking beside Sam, Malivai, Jose, and Tex, hearing the cheers of Unity, Angela, and a whole town. He also had a vision of jogging out for the Yuranigh Magpies and giving Johnno a look and a smile, happy that a best mate was there to share the struggle.

A man stopped them and they waited in the semi-darkness of the tunnel. Ozzie remembered the darkness of his grandfather's death, and of losing a girlfriend and a best mate, as well. He recalled the battle with the demons of the night that followed, a battle that he still hadn't won. For a while he had blamed a lot of people, but Ozzie had eventually realized that unless he forgave he'd never sleep peacefully again. He'd started with himself. If he hadn't been so stupid he'd never have lost Jess, but being stupid was part of growing up, he supposed. And as for Johnno, that thieving bugger, at least he'd apologized. Without that, Ozzie might not be where he was today.

The security guard nodded and Ozzie ran through a large banner. The turf was emerald green and the sunlight dazzling. Ozzie could hear his pop's voice echoing through his head, "C'mon, you gutless wonder. Put in!"

"I will," Ozzie said to himself. "I bloody well will."

acknowledgments

I had a lot of "first" readers for this book: Amanda Rofe, Paul Baker, Mark Massingham, Liz Flynn, Catherine Flynn, and Yvonne Hoerner. Their useful feedback ensures there's a part of each one in this story.

I'm sure many of you would know that Anthony Eaton has a special talent when it comes to writing. He's also a brilliant editor. I can't thank him enough for the work he put into *Out of His League*, and I feel privileged to be on the receiving end of his gift for words and stories.

Leonie Tyle managed the project with her usual aplomb. She finds just the right balance of positivity and constructive criticism—her editing skills are much appreciated. She made sure Ozzie's story wasn't rushed, once again putting an author and a book's best interests in front of making a quick buck.

Thanks also to Felicity McKenzie for her clear and accurate copyediting.

Most of my research for this book took place in the early

1990s, as a student at the University of Texas at Austin. However, reading *Friday Night Lights* by H. G. Bissinger gave me an important insight into what football means to a small town in West Texas. I suggest you read the book before you see the movie. *The Australian Guide to American Football* by Tony Morgan helped me remember what all those positional names, plays, and numbers actually mean.

I received an Arts Queensland grant for this book, for which I'm most grateful.

Thanks to Karen Brooks and Queensland Creative Industries for showcasing the book in New York, and Emily Easton and the team at Walker Books for Young Readers for giving it a new name and a new life.